Charles Akpo
Christopher Bimpeh

Casa City

Charles Akpo
Christopher Bimpeh

Casa City

JustFiction Edition

Imprint
Any brand names and product names mentioned in this book are subject to trademark, brand or patent protection and are trademarks or registered trademarks of their respective holders. The use of brand names, product names, common names, trade names, product descriptions etc. even without a particular marking in this work is in no way to be construed to mean that such names may be regarded as unrestricted in respect of trademark and brand protection legislation and could thus be used by anyone.

Cover image: www.ingimage.com

Publisher:
JustFiction! Edition
is a trademark of
International Book Market Service Ltd., member of OmniScriptum Publishing Group
17 Meldrum Street, Beau Bassin 71504, Mauritius

Printed at: see last page
ISBN: 978-620-0-10726-8

PREFACE

I am thankful indeed to God, and special thanks a lot to all those buying and reading this book. I extend thoughtful compliment and gratitude to all Scholars of Erudition, Intellectuals, and Key Personalities who read this book, contributing to my success. It is more worthwhile, rewarding, edifying, fruitful, fulfilling, heartening, worthy of acknowledgement, if told; you are the key to a person's success. God richly bless you. I pray, the Lord Almighty, to plant you in his heavenly abode. You will grow and bear edible fruits, and succeed in all things. This book draws a line on adventure, along with romance, suspense, and mystery, value of attitude, innovation, interest, lifestyle, intriguing scene, and ideology. It is also on what it takes to liberate the mind from prejudice and ignorance, acting as negative tendencies to development, that must be resolutely solved, and moreover, to consciously discern our actions pervasive of our crisp inner thoughts, to know the consequences of our behaviours. This book intends to edify our minds. The question is what really motivates or gingers the mind to cheat, oppress, mislead, hurt, and carry out wicked acts, to the extent of hurting each other? In any profession one finds himself or herself, only to know in mind, one cannot be without the other, and is about dedication, devotion, being unselfish, reliable, trustworthy, good timekeeping. We can identify each member in the society by dint of his or her name at birth, his status, or position that he occupies, and the role he plays, and so on. Name is a significant piece of equipment very effective to influence our lives. How we perceive what our names mean affect us in a way. We have to let our names work out to our benefits; bearing in mind, we have the same likeness, created in the image of God, in terms of our bodies like trees full of branches, likewise a body with parts. There are bound to be differences on how we see methodology on law, value, belief, aim, aspiration, goal, and achievement, to provide useful insights into issues relating to perception of people that really matters. Immediately a baby comes out at birth when a woman goes into labor, he or she gets a name to carry everywhere, although a person can swear an oath by an affidavit to change a name. We acquire features from our parents, such as height and skin colour. At growth, we learn of emotions, the sum of individual properties that make us unique.

On moral obligation, we acquire values as we interact with people in school, at home, with peer group, in the society, monastery, mosque, and church, with anticipation that, is suppose to enrich our years on earth, and considered necessary to our lives. How long does it take very consciously to discern good from evil? From the day of conception to declining years, life is a voyage of dedication to a sense of purpose. It is about having the quality of knowing and carrying out what is morally right to bring a good reputation. On the occurrence of social peace as well as harmony crucial for the progress of a Country, to aid us live exemplary lives, we learn to authenticate claims on evidence. Life, since creation has been a battlefield for survival, dealing with the challenges that surround us, as we seek a place of refuge where we can be released from the burdens and struggles of this inevitable life into a fortress of success. The insanity of inequality and discrimination hunt our sub consciousness and consciousness, but it takes love to conquer. The chord of love is strong, healing wounds. Love radiates light in our hearts to have a peaceful demeanor. Love is not a betrayer of trust. We wallow not in defeat, but to triumph in strength, with every ounce of human emotion, dwelling on determination, confidence, and boldness. To cope with the hustle and bustle of everyday endeavor, what this present generation needs is attitudinal change, realizing our potentials and working at it to perfection, in arousing the forces of imagination. This book emphasizes on the outcome of our actions on pain, ridicule, and coordination, bringing the word to light, thus becoming more intimately acquainted with everyday life. Since what we normally say conceived in thought, how often are our words yielding changes in our lives? It pays to honor our words with decency, to enable us live a fulfilling life uncontaminated. We learn to take heart in a time of perseverance, speaking the truth, working hard, and reaping bountifully, not to be discouraged when things do not go the way we want. Acting in accordance with destiny, without learning to work together is like growing weeds with wheat. Togetherness can produce progress on a common goal. Our sense of touch must correspond with our sense of thought. We learn not to abhor hatred in our hearts, for the outcome of hatred is murder. Whatever we do carelessly, we live to regret in the future. Patience is the stepping-stone to learn and act carefully. Searching for wisdom, truth, instruction and discernment will enable us, more disciplined to behave sensibly and wisely. When there are important matters to discuss, fools have nothing sensible to say. Life is about choices, be it vital or to our doom, but the end result matters. Life is all about doing the right thing, in the right place at the right time, to recognize our ambitions and to work hard at it, and not to give in to be distracted, thus, to discourage us from reaching goals we have set for ourselves, to use our abilities and talents to the benefit of all and sundry. The heart is a light. It shines in our lives as the eyes to see. Love makes our lives meaningful and practical; it awakens our discernments, our motives, and actions. How many times are we offended when insulted and discouraged, or grateful when corrected and encouraged? We spell out the need to respect opinions of other people. In the story, Animal portrayed as a wicked leader, and he received the result of his wickedness. What does it take to be a leader? Is it to know and defend the rights of his people, to rule with justice, give stability to his nation, and nourish his Citizens in riches? To them that speak before they think, this demonstrates symptom of psychiatric disorder. The Clinic is not too far from where they are, to seek medical help and pray. They are just holding the air or wind in the palms, hardly possible. How can we be of help to others, to connote friendly warmth? How often have we proceeded to solve problems that insidiously hinder progress? The crux of the issue is to ignore such unarguable nonsense when often besieged by monumental mishap and its mass hysteria of abnormality, to enable us live in an aura of peace to subside fury, substantiating evidence for libel claims. As an Author, I write to exhibit my deepest thoughts, stressing on opinion of achievement, hunt for wisdom and knowledge, and to stand out in difficult circumstances. These actually depend on perfect networking and those likely to influence our decisions and to discern solution to a problem. We limit the sense of perspective if we pretend not to face reality when individuals sidelined on the notion that one is not part of the group or very pathetic to society. An unstable mind is the gateway to destruction and brain damage. Precision and certainty to cohere with one view is the headway to strategic goal attainment. To seek advice from achievers is the link leading dreams to maturity. In all things, we ought to be true to ourselves, honest, and to give laudable space to think, explore, and adjust to conditions around us, as a masterpiece and stepping stone to improve our potentials. The way we live our lives exemplify to others our mindsets and priorities, having the insight to govern our instincts, knowing what is right and wrong. Ignorance is a life-threatening disease that can lead one astray, but a curious mind will cure this canker by digesting every utterance to fish out the truth, and to take a firm stand by transforming every situation that will get under our feet. Humiliation and verbal abuse are dangerous killers and pathways to insanity, due to constant worry and nervous tension. When emotional intelligence is deformed, it makes the mind sick; eventually causing harm to the entire body, likewise unachieved desires of the heart makes it ailing. Precision in our words and ways calm despicable annoyance, similarly, a mind at peace and free from worry prolongs lifespan and brings healing. What we think of little value can be a thorn in the flesh.

Not to overcome a fear will surely hunt the conscience. We live to fight battles undefeated, dreadful if it becomes an enormous giant. Our lives often dip into despair when our attentions and intentions dwell on how we want others to see, take into account, and uncover our sensitivities, when we are in a haste to make decisions uncalled in an attempt to please insatiable mandate to do the needs of man. Our philosophies, beliefs, and ideologies inherent in us account for who we are. Matters of the hearts are with little happiness but much sorrows, however, depending on how we live our lives by living within the confines of the law, we will always have a life at amity and accomplishment. As the saying goes, "What the eyes do not see, the heart does not grieve over." When the ears hear, and the eyes see, likewise, our senses activated, they act on our hearts, followed by a signal to the mind to propel an action. This action can be beneficial or disastrous.

The link between heart and mind is our senses acting on our bodies, leading to motion. Hidden feeling is what seen on the outside. The inward man is his action and prolonged expression on explicit issues, come to think of smiling, frowning, and crying that is shown on faces. However, we can be in command of consciousness, the fount of identity, to choose a healthy and reasonable idea, and make an informed ruling on our views deep-rooted in the fabric of society. One way or another, life never treats us how we want it, but we have to steer the innermost entity to materialize on the outside. To bear helpful thoughts and clean mind keep the soul and heart alive. Contents of Casa City are pieces of life worth reading.

Contents

1. TRIP

It was time for execution. Failure is not a choice, as the prisoners did wait for such a moment of intermediate action. They were with every appearance of such a need for a termination of their faith, within a degree of diverse impression written on their faces, contorted in anticipation to sabotage the quintessence of pertinent school of thought, so spurious, about forthcoming execution. The tumbrel or patrol wagon just arrived at the prison gate to transport those condemned to the guillotine. A release cord or a release button releases the blade on the guillotine. There is also a hanging site at the gallows. The Scientists hardly knew would end up in prison. When satellite images depicted an asteroid fallen to the earth, they were determined to trace it. However, before the incidence of imprisonment, theprisoners were Scientists working within the Intelligence Service to strive for answers to seemingly unanswerable questions, cutting across cosmology of astronomical observations in physics, to find antidotes to the complexities of human anatomy, living cells, inquiring into principles permeating all faculties and field of study. Also, knowing why the spirit passes from the body and enters another, actually the transmigration of a dead soul into another, which is a force that transcends the ordinary laws of nature. Additionally, delved into different conditions experienced in the habitat of cell organelles surrounded by cell membranes, the essence of kingdoms and nerve cells specialized for transmitting electrical messages within the body. Moreover, the Scientists examined the cytology of stem cells from humans or animals, that when incorporated within cytoplasmic, protoplasmic, and nucleus of dead cells, living cells can be accepted and enabled to grow for a useful scientific purpose, the same in allotransplantation, cloning, and the taxonomy of living organisms. Their researches were to advance a theory and formulate hypothesis; Argue and develop a thesis to admit or reject; Conduct analysis; Make prediction; Design an experiment; Make observations; Consider, interpret and scrutinize their findings; And draw conclusions before presenting it out. They made out some of the planets had minerals in them that can be mined. Far away in outer space of the galaxies are meteors that looked like planets and additional planets. As the Scientists felt something unusual from their navigation systems, they looked engrossed in thoughts with such intense gravity, with amazing and awe-inspiring facts, not to drift away from their main source of focus. This unusual feeling was phenomenal. Focused on satisfying their curiosities, they were plagued by the itch to go beyondtheir abodes, a seemingly simple idea to achieve their goals, which was seen as an opportunity to meet all sorts and classes of humanity and wished their inner drives will pull them from the depth of despair and misery. Talented Academicians looked to the future for utopian world, but only found in delusion, prediction, visualization, forethought, farsightedness, and imagination. Following the signal, they went on an expedition, and were on board a ship. Gripped with anxiety, it was the most imperative endeavor of their lives to embark on a tortuous and perilous trip.

Their hearts in the midst of burning light were full of thoughts to bring forth what is in them; the ardent craving to unearth their potentials, devoted to duty, and dependable to plough back confusing situations for a change. In addition, to let the radiating light of love in their paths sparkle, filling their souls with true inspirations of truth, enabling them grow in knowledge and wisdom, united in spiritand mind on a common cause.

They rolled out to sea ambitiously. The Scientists were also branded, the T.B.A. for their work. The reality beyond the obvious is to face the fact to emphatically gratify and accomplish the things that mean the most. It was a perfectly lovely morning when the sun burst openly through the cloud, appeared as though about to scorch with intensity. The air looked lovely to bear the beauties of nature. Suddenly, stable mass of cumulus cloud covered the atmosphere and scudded across the sky. The sun hid invisibly as the cloud enfolded the bright skies. The sky frowned and went vilely. Billows of gushing wind vandalized along the tidal waves of the ocean. Thunder lambasted its gigantic sound to scare the hearts of those on board the ship. The clouds discharged electricity. Then, there was an electrifying bolt of lightning to usher in a raging torrent of rain. Later the rain subsided as the clouds dissolved in the sky. Arc of a rainbow manifested in the skies. Flock of birds with a flap of their wings wheeled past a distance with their delightful songs. Before the rain, the T.B.A. sought a roof over their heads in the cabin, huddling for warmness. The T.B.A. cultivated the propensity for drinking and quaffed soft drinks, hard liquor, and gin mixed with lemon. They also sipped hot tea and coffee that ultimately burnt their mouths, while others took it in a gulp. It was a sainted patience of anxiety, perhaps going to places to remember their miseries no more. They were beginning to thrash their arms against the cold and craned their necks to catch the first glimpse of land as they approached the coast; itching to wander in an unknown land as they made a landfall on the seaside. Their faces lit with gladness. Abina was ecstatic at the outcome as that of a wedding occasion when a ring was twisted on her finger. However, prediction was not the obvious. Unknown to them, this destination was hard to find on the map, but that notion altered with their presence. Casa City was a place of no return and a land out of the ordinary in speech and language until Military intrusion. The Casians intercepted every boat that strolled within their territorial waters. To them, that is tantamount to an invasion of unwanted species trying to cause havoc. Then, out of nowhere, Bang! Bang! The ship shook in a bizarre circumstance, a haywire of chaos, an overwhelming pandemonium. A missile struck to torpedo the ship. The law of the jungle had its way. The Captain of the ship fired a gun that displayed bright light in the atmosphere to signal danger. With a huge voice, he declared, "Ladies and gentlemen, we are experiencing some difficulties with extreme turbulence. If you can flee, do so, but make sure to use the lifeboat. It is likely there is feeling of killer sharks and whales ready to have you and would not spare an inch of a time." The missile came from a submarine belonging to the Casians. Speedboats were nearing them. Those who attempted to throw themselves overboard were caught regrettably. The Coast Guards mounted on the ship to bring them along the shore before the ship sank into the heart of the sea, and then took up power. The exertion of force seized them. The T.B.A. was highly scrutinized. On the verge of one of them asking why such an attack, he was met with a slap that twirled him around. The pain seared across his face. The Scientist got enraged. "Oh God, heart of patience, please." He prayed within as he gnashed his teeth vindictively. His colleagues signaled to him to remain calm, if not, only to worsen their plights. The Coast Guard's huge physique never frightened him. He would have caught him unaware by targeting his synovial joints, making initial attempt to dislocate it, and rip him limb from limb. An Official from the Castle moved toward Dorothy, attempted to molest her, after expressing warmth of herattractive body. She became tense, ill at ease, apprehensive, and nervous. She swallowed hard a drop of saliva. Her soft drawling voice attempted to fight back. It was a taboo for men to touch women indecently with veils until married. This Official had no respect for culture, taken by lust to gratify his immediate desire. He sniffed her tidy hair with much endorsement, then sucked smoke from a cigar into his mouth and let it out on her face. "Hey, she is mine!" Samuel burst out in fury. The Official came close to him and smote him so hard. He head butted Samuel's nose, gripped him by the neck and threw him down, attempting to chock him with all his strength. Samuel tried to wrestle his strength out of his possession. He hit the Official continuously in the face with his fist. A Guard intervened, "Enough! He will face the music in prison for his bloody mouth utterances. We will be parents to them to teach them how to respect if that escaped their minds sincechildhood." It was an insult to Samuel's intuition to resolve the matter, at the same time disarmed, with their belongings seized. A truck arrived and a cold, hard faced man with thick eyelashes and sunken eyes, holding a loaded gun got near to them to articulate his evil intent, but outwardly posed as a man of hospitality, a diffusion of illusion, and facing reality on a memorable surge of self-esteem. He glanced at length towards them, and then grinned evilly. All he stipulated was to make sure none left out of view. The power of the gun renders one in submission. He then probed their presence on their soil. He said, "Now we are going to play a game. I offer you a choice-life or death. One of you will be chosen to shoot six of you for his life to be saved and the rest of the crew. Then, the one who shot the six of you will play hide and seek with nine of us. We go into hiding while he looks for us. Is that clear!?" "Not yet," Oneof the T.B.A. answered. "Hey you look here! Come here and explain yourself!" he raised a stinging command. At that moment, terror blurred their thoughts. He went to him and said, "Nothing to explain Sir." "Is that so? Oh, well, you will know what it takes to explain." He gave the order and the T.B.A. was flogged four times in the chest, and then given the gun to do as told. Actually, the VIPERS put him to the test if he will either shoot his friends or the VIPERS, as they intentionally loaded the gun with rubber bullets in their presence. A twinge of nervousness seized him. He shook while he aimed the gun at his colleagues, one after the other. He negotiated in thought as to shoot or not. Faces forced tears out and took on a sad note. "Don't shoot us please," they pleaded. One of the VIPERS who always suck his thumb in the mouth in place of food gloated, "Ha! Ha! Ha! He does not have what it takes to bleed a fowl. He is bred by growth hormones." Another also teased, "Did you miss your Mum and Daddy? I dare you to shoot!" "No!" He voiced out loud and dropped the gun to the ground. The one who gave the gun to him said, "Well, you passed the test not shooting at us. We will not kill you either. Move this way!" The T.B.A. was manacled. The Scientists were away in the truck, while chivvied to comply defiantly, as the door slammed in their faces to see the leader at the Castle. On the way, the T.B.A. saw impressive buildings, which sit right on the sea front that looked isolated from the main City of Casa. The infallible edifice emanating from the influx of water gushing from the waterfall was very attractive. The roads were narrow and broad, leading off the ocean highway with well-decorated houses, which lie back from the road, having street names and house numbers with colorful flowers. Flags waved above the City square. The truck halted at an iron gate, which automatically opened. The Scientists then walked up along an empty shady pathway to the hall of the Castle and saw stone effigies of lions, tigers, snakes, and leopards. The Castle Guards threw insults in their faces. The T.B.A. suppressed the rage of fury to the derision and insult targeted at them, praying earnestly within for heavenly involvement. At the awaited moment to analyze their faith, a very tall man, quite brewed in years with grey hat came stalking gorgeously along. He stared at them and frowned to show wrinkles on his face. He later took off his hat, revealing his receding hair. His hair carefully cropped to match the bald at the top of his forehead, and his eyes clear and large. His scalp was so unfriendly to grant him the grace of hair; nevertheless, he had the capacity of an intelligent man. His nice perfumed body was pleasant smelling. He looked on with an unusual solemnity of expression. He waggled his head scornfully, then smirked, trying to show a sign of dignity and hospitality in his smile, but sinister within.

He seemed lost in favor with humanity. Mostly stammers when talking which sometimes prompts pain to his broken nose. Anytime speech impediment seizes him, one can prepare a meal before he utters the next word. He spoke to the Scientists, disdainful of their mindsets, "what on earth, are you doing here, you such caliber of humans who are likely to face the full rigors of our laws? You have trespassed on the land of forbidden kingdom." The Scientists explained their missions on documentation. He ordered for plantain and egg stew to be served to the Scientists, then wrote a statement and handed it over to a colleague with obvious microscopic stature, thin legs, and tiny neck as of a horn, who in his own words, wrote annoying statements, depicting their field trip was nothing but on grounds of espionage and submitted. Honestly, the Guards were very worried about his thin body and pined for nature to grant him piece of flesh. He has hazy eyes with thick eyebrows, long moustache, goatee beard with strong chin, and soft cheeks. With such lean stature, his movement cast a slur on his moral fiber, as though the weakest wind might knock him down. Nevertheless, he disputed this wrong impression by weight lifting. That was the beginning of their woes. He was finding it hard to agree to their mission. They were also interested to perform scientific research of the asteroid, to extract explicitly, specific meaning to outer space. Their ideas might seem interesting to Animal who is likely to ignore his own research team and get along with them, to put across the perfect expertise on difficult tasks. He later came to order them to the leader. When Animal, who was then the leader of Casa City, absorbed the infuriating remarks of the letter after casting his eyes over the document, he stared at it in utter disbelief, calling their candors into question. Not even an ample plea could have filled Animal's curiosity. Resentment leads tohatred. A revulsion concern swept over his mind, a frozen feeling of repugnance. Animal summoned a meeting. As they conferred together, the Scientists made sense of a problem cropping up. He took a long incredulous hard look at them, and then looked them up and down contemptuously and deliberately as his eyes strayed from the head to the feet and back once more, "So, you came here to spy. What do we have in common, huh! Ok, we shall see. Anyway, you do not look like dumb asses, as told. Am I right?" He exclaimed. What he said was outside the confines of reason to the unthinkable, since it does not sound clear in the ears, as that of someone out of his mind and foolish. Stupidity is not by birth. It is the evil craving of anyone who shuns wisdom, knowledge, and understanding. The Scientists never uttered a word, but that fury on their faces can blow up into bits, Animal's iniquitous brains, and anything. Animal had absolute trust in whatever his Advisor said. His extreme dislike took his eyes off them. The Scientists were terrified as chill seeped through their skins. Their faces turned deathly insipid. That hostile look terrified them. A long face fell before them. Chorus of disapproval revealed on their faces. Animal ordered for their imprisonment, where they were manhandled. Every head was shaved and beard trimmed. Outrageous discrimination was meted out. Where in space will they air their complaint? Even, a baby learns how to talk in the womb, assimilating what the mother says. Anyone who misbehaved stubbornly received a very sound beating. Their bodies always tingle with pain. How can we end man's inhumanity to man? At the maximum-security prison grounds, shouting was strictly forbidden by Wardens at times, except an inmate who was in labor screamed for help. The Scientists recognized other inmates with different categories of crimes, ranging from murder to sexual assault. Others were just like them, tourists who wanted to please their eyes with the most beautiful sentiments of nature, only to be demoralized. They felt condemned to a life of servitude, which curiously enough, postulated a complete submission against their will, completely handicapped morally, mentally, physically, emotionally, spiritually, and academically. Many have learned to live with pain, and theirs were no exception. Kept in solitude deprives one of fundamental human rights and justice, curtailing aim, goal and aspiration. When lost in touch with the grips of descent living, society shuns shattered destiny, only left to bear the stigma of being a convict in the sense of criminality, although exonerated with vindictive proof of innocence. The Scientists waited in patience, though beaten and inflicted, they should accept all in submission. Life goes on at all cost; hardly to correct errors committed in the past, but to learn from it so as not to repeat them again. Thisportrayed their inability to be nice to the advisor to Animal deep in their minds. They brooded over such confrontation sedately. The Wardens inflicted injuries on them, and maimed other inmates. Now could scarcely stand for the thought of being cooped up in solitary confinement. Several days elapsed and getaway eluded them, as they wished for an intervention, and had now recognized it was inevitable to connive with the Wardens. The Wardens were determined to clip their wings to make them get loss of touch with the outside world, restricted their own volition, mistreated further than the ability to endure. Empathy sought assistance in angry cloud. The T.B.A. seemed puzzled about what it means to have a real purpose in life, where there is no need to always argue or fight over unnecessary things, to show love, kindness, sympathy and mutual agreement toward others, to have happiness and contentment in life. They had in mind, kept in solitaryconfinement will not always be the end of them and the reward of forbearance to the end is resounding success, to enable them face the future without a limit to undue perplexities. In the morning, they were released to have fresh air in the open yard surrounded by electrocuting walls. The prisoners mingled work with social activities, and were kept busy with athletics, softball, cycling, soccer, volley ball, netball, basket ball, tennis, hockey, rugby, baseball, cricket, swimming, and also engaged in boxing, wrestling, bowling, and different kinds of sports. In addition to sports, they were also allowed to equip their brains, studying and acquiring skills, attending classes with teachers ready to lecture them. You can find palm trees along the corners of the pillars. At night, the skies are filled with sparkling stars; the sun sets in across the horizon, the moon's sudden appearance, so amazing, then the guards locked them up, but something unusual kept going on at the prison, andthey are yet to experience it. Things not common to human way of life, but will have to dwell on mechanisms to be victorious. Perhaps their search for freedom is likely on the way. They almost threw in the towel, living in constant suspense, filled with dread, and burdened with anxious minds, with eyes weary with longing; hardly to give up the zeal for freedom, to live in harmony without reference to cultural background, ethnic group, tribe or color. It never crossed their minds ending up this way. Life is full of uncertainties, to the extent that, it is even a risk to live, notwithstanding when to err on the side of caution, oh, hmmm... You reach old age with somnolent eyes, only to count your deeds and analyze your past. Affliction of the heart makes it sick. On account of any death in the prison, the dead was speared, and then spared to his faith before burnt to ashes. Unfortunately, Inmates were buried alive for no reason. Such enigmatic behaviour wasincomprehensible. An excruciating gut wrenching torture was unbearable. The choicest were left on top of a mountain, at the crest of a hill in a shrine a day for mountain birds of prey to have their share, before burnt or fed to wild animals, hence the possibility of feigning death to escape was ruled out. The noose of death came to a standstill only when one is set free. They tried to talk themselves out of their situations with much temperate and touching word, as indignant at the outcome, weighed down even if with a cinch to return safe and sound, only to conceive an idea as they waited wholeheartedly for a way out. It is not in the right sense to corrupt our level of judgment with infertile conducts. Our pious life suffers spiritual decay when the flesh subdues the mind and the body. When alone, the Scientists buried their heads in their laps, weeping, as had exhausted all the possibilities. Although the Scientists swallowed ridicule all along,now disheartened victims at the whim of circumstance, a glimmer of anticipation lit their faces to reinforce the lapse of lassitude, to a day we call cessation of enmity. One of the T.B.A. conceived and delivered in the Prison.

2. MEETING

The Intelligence service comprised of members within the Security Service. The navigators in the control room, a section of the science laboratory, which monitored proceedings, were trying to initiate contacts with the Scientists and were emitting signals of their destination. "There could be danger as 'Casa City' can be on the brink of war accelerating" McDonaldson said confusedly, as if, surrounded by dead people. He informed the members in the laboratory at that time. Mr. President got the news and a meeting was to convene immediately to deploy Forces. This issue came in the pipeline, a thought provoking one of course, and demanded drastic measures to thrash it out. He knew in an attempt to ask for pardon to liberate his own, Animal will tamper compassion with reprisal. He might bridle at the suggestion, and will almostnot budge the closest break on them released. The seemingly arguable dispensation of conflicting motion must freeze before escalation, as far as Animal fomented unrest. Before the meeting, another ship was dispatched with Medical Personnel, to cruise along the coast to have a look out, scouting the land, and assessing the strength of its people, to carry out reconnaissance of insurgency. At a far distance to Casa City, the crew mounted telescopes, looked through binoculars, and saw dead bodies washed ashore.

Asimi, one of the prisoners had a hearing device hidden around her thigh, this she managed sneaking to the prison. She established connection and knowledge of their whereabouts known for private conversation to go on unnoticed. They were taught to keep their lips sealed. She was trying to give a complete description of the place, likely signals to aid their locations. A pair of spectacles screened hereyes. A Warden, after screwing his neck around to maintain restriction of movement, with inquisitive mind, came within reach of her, when he recognized she was behaving strangely as if talking to herself. He glared askance at her with an air of nosiness. If he concluded of her insanity, her madness will lead her to the grave to catch sight of paradise and get the drift of the place. Asimi recognized he was drawing near and pretended to sing. The Warden looked intently at her, surveyed her movement and posture. She portrayed a hint of smile looking on, winking her eyes, but could read on his face fuming with madness, taking notice of the burning eyes staring hard at her, a look of exasperation. "Are you in your right mind?" He asked bluntly. Asimi considered his stream of statement very abusive. She itched with an inquisitive mind. "Ask yourself that question. What do you mean by that? Hope you are far from being insane instead. I am a Psychiatrist. You are not of yourself aren't you?" She demanded while snobbish. Her hard-nosed statement cut him deeply. He pointed the gun to his head in contemplation, cocked it to scare the hell out of her, and then waited for his conscience to give him the command to shoot. "Shut the fucking hell up, or else, I will blow out your membranes! I am damn sure about that!" He yelled. He took umbrage at her remark. She had the temerity to question him. Humanity each time complicates a simple matter. Only yes or no answer is all. At least this torment to have the muzzle right on the scalp to scatter her brains out would not have occurred. Such an unusual feature was grueling to comprehend an obvious sign of anomaly. It was a long time she saw her Trichologist. The Warden exhibited no respect for compassion. He had the gut to put a gun to his head. She reflected this words thoughtfully, "God of Abraham, Isaac, and Jacob, please where are you?" Twitch of nervousness overtook her, butshe played tricks on him to consume his time. Asimi spoke in a very soft tone of voice, calling for sanity to prevail, a voice to the voiceless, "It is not your fault, you were not brought up well" She bleated. His huge voice answered with cold remarks and with clenched teeth, "Mind your language woman before I steam you like frozen chicken left to thaw and then throw it to the dogs. I said keep quiet, huh, and how many times should I tell you that! The next cutting word out of your mouth will be the end of you. Is that clear?" He turned nasty. She mumbled, "Yes please." He went on, "Who asked you to come here, anyway? Is it your great grandmother or grandfather? Do you want to have your brains as a delicacy to vultures? Why question my integrity?" Asimi kept engaging him in dialogue, "Does pain mean anything to you? I know my rights." His harsh words went with a smack, "Is that so! Ok, free yourself. Your trial and tribulation will finish here to the natural order of things done in our premises." She reacted tearfully to talk her way out of what might befall her, "For heaven's sake, please show compassion on this body. Don't you like it, eh?" She begged with trembling mouth in an attempt to throw herself at him while she positioned her breasts well for observation and posing sexy. Awkward dismay made her voice tensed with indignation. Beguiling persona hid her intimate reaction, shrieking in terror. Shrill run down her veins. It turned scary as shaken to the bone. How can she figure out a moderate reaction to an angry confrontation with a chiseled face? She orchestrated every detail to pacify him. Her knees began to knock. He took the gun off. She passed water, peeing on herself. She was pissed off with his way of behaviour. His presence irritated her. Indescribable numbness stirred up in her. The expression on his face transformed into mere exasperation. Kind gesture struck his psyche, concentrating on theneed to retreat. He then left to attend to duties, but instructed her to come with him, whistling as he went to enjoy his meal. She sighed, then drew out her tongue and hooted in silence. At long last, she found the way to his heart, and to his mode of thought. What went on did strike the Warden like thunderbolt. Although he kept on brooding over her statement, he managed to scare the hell out of her anyway, with no sense of gratification, but of displeasure. Taking innocent life was meaningless. Better safe than sorry, self-reproach had to give way to a purposeful life. Sitting around formations of long circular tables were very eminent Scholars, Members of the Security Council, Cabinet, Judges, and Distinguished Personalities. This issue incumbent on them had assumed an air of significant consideration to call a dead end to exploitation and incarceration, and will scarcely give in tothe slightest compromise. Mr. President was then escorted in and he received a couple of salute from the Officers. One might assume what sort of ideas they were battling with, as seemed deeply in thoughts. Perhaps their instincts unravel the mysteries of the mind, hardly enough to obliterate in retrospect the sharp recollection of all the participants and with a drive to enforce loyalty, law, and order. The President's massive voice pierced through the air and the heart of the gathering. Then he spoke with profound alacrity, "my Distinguished Personalities, the die is cast. The action is now or never. The time has come to step in and put our Experts in charge of this critical mission. We are about to embark on an invasion of Casa City, and having those with deep and rich experience in combat. The slightest attempt to use force and aggression will trigger annoyance to an obvious bone of contention, and the so-called Animal and his wife Tania will flame up a shatteringviolence, hardly to succumb side by side in a compromise. This will put our Scientists in danger. We have to demystify an iota of truth, to accede to the fact that, everything goes according to systematic plan to thwart the effort of these ants; to have fact finding methods rooted in mental acuity, and foresight of unique mind. We have to play logical truancy to their brains to serve as an insult to their emotions. Our men are going out there and we have to support them with a yardstick to determine the fundamental principles of inspiration. Let us examine this blood of humankind, not allowing anything to turn us aside from set of purpose." He expressed his opinions candidly and his arguments were cogent at the decisive meeting to effect much influence on what people believe, depicting one of a vibrant and charismatic leader. The President continued with his speech, "It might seem to suppose we have to seek out the facts and let them fall where they might not be taken for granted. There is emphasis on a hidden perpetuity of truth buried deep at the back of our minds and we treat such with much scrutiny. We have to teach them societal values and systems of diligence, honesty, and integrity. Teach them to speak rightly and have clear conscience of discernment. In addition, to have sure hope, discipline, and show respect in their speech, and obey instruction. Our motive is to complete the assignment and get out unharmed. We want Animal dead or alive for gross massacre and human rights abuse! On this note, I declare a bounty on his head!" A member of the Security Council also reacted solemnly and emphatically, "We have to make sure to embed and enhance stability of their minds, an epitome of norms, to help them think like intellectuals, to acquire knowledge and skills, preparing them for the future. How can we be indifferent to the plights of ourown?" Views were expounded openly. The President signed the death warrant, taking effect immediately. It was a heated discussion, tension very high to reach a consensus. It is indisputable fact that, men and women to carry out the mission were of the highest intellect to conjure up every hidden agenda, were admirable personalities who never wasted thoughts upon their dignity, and with fine acute mind, possessing exceptional strength, in capable hands those with military prowess. As the meeting was ending, the educated elite weighed in with the views of all the influential speakers, mostly with noble consistency to digest the information discreetly. These were intelligent and cultivated personalities and dignitaries refined with a look of sophistication, with such gentle outlook and seemingly sufficient with credentials of humanity, on noble dispensation with deeper and logical insight into essence of reality. The meeting concluded inunanimity. As they concentrated on bare facts to deal with the situation, they were also aware of being entrusted with the well-being of Citizens, really cut out for leadership, with modest demeanor to solve the problems hindering the progress of their people, especially, poverty. One serious indication of poverty is to make you forget your own name and even your children. When underprivileged, being alive every morning makes life irritating. The needy most often attracts illness while not ill and uncomfortable situations, thereby smearing them inferior. Poverty-stricken does not disqualify one with the embodiment of knowledge. Moral decay and deception are contributing factors stifling development, when sense of honor invaded by selfishness. Only because those invested with power, not because, are not up to their tasks, nor surrounded by ineffective Advisors, but sake of being reluctant, thus, refusing to acknowledge the need for improvement. In such state of affairs, having unfair advantage tends to render inoperative the needed developmental outline. Everyone yearns to crossover from a state of hopelessness to affluence to protect a sense of identity. Things obvious and standard of living depicted by the people attest to itself. The reality to afford comfort is to have the means in this wild pace of life. Salt City was economically active and efficient when it comes to work. Strict adherence to work enforced. Cost of commodities and rendering of services were at reasonable prices. Governance is to weigh the concerns of the citizens, to accomplish them on a scale of preference, with a strong sense of belonging to propel a nation forward looking. Besides, it asks for a balance in an idea and performance, instead of being long on ideas and short on performance. It is easier to elaborate much on a manifesto than implementation, as to what we usually say, "Talk the talk, andwalk the walk." If there is an enabling platform, where Citizens can air their grievances to a committee in all constituencies, where annually, or immediately, an account of what expected of them is given, Leaders can always be abreast of the state of the nation. Since a Leader cannot sweep around the whole Country every day, the committee can hold people accountable for deficiencies, and then hand them over to Officers. Building a nation is a corporate responsibility from the corridors of power to the wretched beggar at the church, monastery, mosque, and on the street, where we see ourselves as solution to problems. There is a state of anomy and very problematic when suffering is assumed as part and parcel of the populace to portray a situation as all right and tolerable. The vast knowledge, in its entirety, is mostly capable of making every effort to push us out of limitations, provided we are not complacent about our deplorable conditions of living, if not, a country will always be stuck in a warp, stifling progress. We abuse and grieve the mind when it lies idle. You feed a lazy hand by empowering it with resources and the needed strength for his feet to work and breed money, then, you teach a beggar how to give, and to kick them out of their uncomfortable beds. Honesty is one of the bedrocks to development and national consensus.

3. CASA CITY

Casa City is a mountainous region, andwith plane scenery that might seem she is isolated from civilization. That is not the case. She is a nice Crypto-City, can almost be categorized as a Country, with well planned topography, safeguarded, and considering the astronomical cost of building, money has been put into reasonable use to acquire the Cadillac immensity of fortified fortresses, stonking with stylish interior décor. In addition, glamorous palaces, mansions, castles, high-rise or story buildings, bungalows, sky scrapers on wide outskirts with broad streets. Casa City abounds in affluence, extravagance, and sensual pleasures, thus acknowledged fully as a magnificent composite of a modern city. Her survival intertwined with alarming frequency, having grand industrial landscape. She has clean environment, clean water, and a vast expanse of land for farming, with typical forest areas. Natural resources abound in this area, and almost believed to emerge from the Ocean, where, when viewed afar it looked like typical concentration of smoke and fire, but baffling to observe the beauty of nature when near, as the place glowed. You could find fragrant flower plantation, cultured in a biodiversity environment. A railway line has been constructed from the coast to the city. The underground rail lines mostly linked to the mining sites, nucleus of major businesses, companies, and their research base. It serves as the route to the submarine, and provides perfect source of escape in times of war. A man named IQ and his sailors with teams of Archaeologists and Anthropologists discovered her during an adventure spree centuries ago. As the years went on, children multiplied. Numerous events spanned a long period. IQ bestowed much affection on them and contributed immensely to the development of Casa City; bearing in mind, key to success periodically dwells in a capacity worth risking. The Citizens hardly lacked anything, as the yardstick of adecent living kept improving. Subsequent succession of leaders surfaced as many years elapsed, until, the turn of the dictator, Animal, assuming the mantle of leadership. He was with radical viewpoint, and brought much skepticism to the surrounding region, which accelerated more and more, until it grew complex. Animal had a strong voice and a wistful look. He had perforated his two ears, having earrings as long as his elongated neck, which actually drew much strength on his temple. Due to his age, he was at then a grey haired man and with steely eyes, muscular chest, and powerful body. He has a heavy moustache almost covering his mouth. The need to be in full gear cast a slur and aspersion on his motive, a man of dignity in his own eyes. He was always consumed with anger, which drew deep lines on his facial expression. Animal lacked acts of diplomacy. A strange unnatural human being easily hurt and upset, lost in an immensely abundantbrain, unforeseen tumult to his debility, which had neither a scientific proof nor a philosophical training, and by constant learning of natural aptitude alike, looked much inferred by subjective standards of truth, extremely problematic. This as a result, prompted him to let out his burning anger to consume. He was always suspicious, like a victim of a doubtful mind, yearning to know the cause of his pessimism, and always consumed by a longing for recognition, to determine his action to reaction. Animal lived in a nightmare, and constant fear of an uprising. His humor in retrospect was undeterminable, oscillated between happiness and despair. Other disquieting circumstances threw doubt on his manner of behavior, very cruel and violent, where he will never wish you a flock of apology when at fault, which made him proud in his unaffected air of complete amiability that brought him weighty relief. Rapped about in elaboration of cynical gesturesand tyranny in disguise, he regarded his fellow subjects with false pretense, unruffled by the sharpest and most contrary judgment of his people. His guilt ridden conscience sometimes caused him grief and shared tears that knew no bounds. Anyone who knew him very well was himself and his self esteem. His wife, Tania was no exception to be precise. She had an awkward sense of humor, a blatant liar and mischievous. Her means of disdainful conduct was questionable. Always known to shout to make her presence felt due to her quick temper. She had a tragic mind during her childhood and as she managed to keep the lid on her illicit affair, Tania was subjectively awarded for promiscuity. Her unique make-up buried her wrinkles. Tania's stiff-necked attitude made her unique in her own eyes, which she used to pollute her husband's brain with negativeimaginations, where she regarded herself of very high importance as she always strode forward in pride. It was always obvious she lied through her teeth. On one occasion, Tania sat astride a chair; gold rings adorned her fingers, and much excited with an affectionate smile and gazed at her husband reclining contentedly in a chair. For the sake of her height, her legs hardly touched the ground. Nonetheless, her high heels eased height augmentation. Although she had a stunt growth in height, that never interrupted her sharp brains. She was always nervous to sit still for more than a minute at a time. As difficult and arrogant as he was, she tried to influence her husband. Tania knew Animal's weak spot to get him at her fingertips. Size was no barrier to her, not at all. She frequently interrupted Animal's plans to distract his attention as she took on the man of the house to instruct her husband to differentiate his left from right. After giving him a conclusive night of enjoyment, it creates the grounds to coax him into agreeing to her demands. Who was even there to warn him of this corrupted mind? She fanned herself majestically. Then, Tania went to him and sat by him. She could tell by the look on his face he was troubled. He stroked her underarm. She enquired curiously, "Why are you perplexed, puzzled, and having lots of confusion bothering your mind, as if you want to carry the whole world on your head? I have on recognition; you are always awake all the time in bed. Be a strong man; capitalize your weakness with wickedness. Be strong, fearless, violent, and brutal. Torment psychologically your opponents, and let them know you are as wild as a ferocious lion." She infected him with harmful words, and Animal obliged like an animal led to the slaughterhouse. No doubt, women have been endowed with hidden beauty in clothes and on faces that seem to subdue men. His quick intent look cut her nerves, making herdiscontented on edge. Animal's adamant and unbending heart of rock crushed at her feet when led to her loins. Tania herself on several occasions ordered massacre in her husband's name, as she yearned to occupy the center of attention, residing in ideological lawlessness and treachery. She targets, especially women who might look attractive to her husband, took a fleeting glance at them, then finds fault with everything they do, even the air they breathe. She traps them, ensnares their paths, and accuses them falsely before the close associates of Animal, then were forcefully fed to lions and crocodiles. She threw her weight around to malign anyone who stood her way. Her misbehaviour threw doubt on her genuineness. She could not stand a day of not causing harm, which was indelibly engraved upon her brain. Act of betrayal at times flew her into rage, as that of anyone spellbound by the gods of Ouagadougou and its repercussions. She loved to watch such pleasant sight of violence at the slightest provocation, and was full of pretension on conceit. Animal was living with a woman he detested actually. He was led and bedeviled by her beauty, sticking to what is pleasing to the eyes, and even to the extent of being instructed on how to comb his hair. To lay out a matriarchal home, then there is gross concern when men's strength woven underarm with hair stuck out. Marriage never last when it bases on lust and the whole mindset not right. Instead, it is common among people to feed on mere cohabitation. There is the need to uphold the significance of marital decency. When a man finds a woman after his own heart, or a woman finds a man after her own heart, marriage is deep-rooted in a never-ending gladness, appreciation, and satisfaction, notwithstanding any condition. One day, adorned with gleaming minerals, Tania walked in the garden of Animal to have fresh air, normally done on weekends, but this time, it was late in the night. Her eyes saw something remarkable. She hid from view and peeped anxiously, perhaps mistaken Animal for somebody else. "Oh no, it is Animal." she exclaimed. Animal was having a high-quality time with a woman. He was actually making love to her. She swallowed saliva quickly, as if her mouth burnt of pepper, finding it difficult to stand on her feet. Obviously, something was wrong. Tania was not of herself, as she begrudged their intimacy. Tania took notice of the woman, Owusua, and marked her for death. She gave them a cold sardonic glare. Why treated this way, was it because she was outmoded and no more in the beauty cycle? Was she disengaged to body alignment and shapeless? Is it because whisky is different from brandy? Not at all, for men with their unquenchable appetites will demand for more whatever they set eyes on. It is of the essence and of necessity to havecontentment in between the silky legs of a woman when married, but not to mix soup and stew, although hard to abide by such rules. One can prepare soup and stew discretely. Marriage breakdown much dwelt on mere dissatisfaction and misunderstanding. Resentment generated evil thought, as Tania reacted with fury, very sour when tasted on the tongue, which generated an act to malign and look down on Owusua. She gave way for her deviant behaviour to carry her along, angling for attention. Tania wondered what women saw, so enticing, to draw them to him. She ought to find that formula bringing about the very strong attraction. It is worth a try to tell him how she felt. However, she should count herself lucky to stay long with him. He is well known to marry for duration of two days.

Later in the week, Tania sent for Owusua with a beautiful flower and a note, reading of her to meet Tania at the Grave Garden late in the night, acting in a fit of rage. She is to come alone while given route to follow, stating that, she wanted her as personal assistant. Without any hint of trap set for her, that was the only split second of Owusua's days on earth. She got to the Grave Garden, felt insecure walking alone after dark, and without informing anybody. Honestly, the woman could barely make out a figure in the darkness of the night. What should have struck her conscience was to beware of lonely streets, to wear an insightful mind to figure out her hidden agenda. She could not find Tania. Her shrilled voice went for her name. However, Tania's reluctance to answer simply fanned her weird nervousness, her spirit then troubled and tumbled to the possibility of being ensnared. Then the notion to meet her very late at night sounded absurd.

Deception held a victim captive. All along, she should have figured out Tania's ulterior motive. Unknowingly, Tania was watching her, glancing around, and rolling her eyeballs like an owl aiming at its target to kill, to see if she came alone. Thoughts of battering Owusua drained her mind. She crept up on her and smashed her face with an object, striking her down from behind deliberately. Owusua fell lifeless. Tania hastily smothered her, killing the woman in the process. Owusua's trachea shrank. She gouged out her eyes and dragged her to where the lion's den was, threw her to the lions that mauled her flesh. Tania bundled out of the place hurriedly to the Castle before Animal came looking for her, while she rightly left the flustered woman as though in her analysis to bobble in her agony. Not even a remorseful sign of passion, rather a heartless air of animosity, apathetic to the plight of sorrow and pain. Two days later, Animal was wondering why the newfound love not seeing him. He sent for her but she was nowhere in sight, after presuming she might turn up. An intensive search ordered until it proved futile. All along, Tania displayed ahypocritical leniency and very concerned, as though she lost a dear one. The burden of guilt hunted her; ate into her until her last breath. A tormented mind hardly flees from a murderer. It paints the brains until death, hard to cherish the goodwill of sleeping with sweet dreams.

As Animal sat under a tree enjoying the cool breeze sunny day, served with chilled tea and slices of bread, and relieving his conscience in such a very calm repose, pondering over matters spoken by Tania, his countenance turned horrifying,distorting, scary, shocking, petrifying, and disturbing. His head sank forward on his chest and he looked like one admitted in thought. He knocked his head several times; think…think…think…think…think…think. The snare of a sorcerer seemed to subdue him. Beguiled by obsession with unseen deity holding sway over his life, he yearned for power desperately, but never woke up without finding life more insignificant,than it was a day before. For the past was once before the future. He felt very much disgusted as if in psychosomatic torment of mystical uncertainties full of immortals struggling to have a hold over his life. Animal ought to yield to a redemptive power beginning with repentance. That would have been his salvation and deliverance. His mouth kept muttering in thought, "A demonic hatred is brewing mischief within." As if, his lips lacked refinement and firmness, so unseasonable to assert dominance over tainted vanity, for nothing else mattered when alone, only a reflection of an unseen shadow, and If he had known, that is the time he should have prayed to overcome it. His burning eyes longed for moisture to hide a murdering face. After all, it occurred to him there was no future, and this made him lose his temper. A mighty blazing light ought to outstrip the abyss of imperial darkness with utmost intensity. He must be a conqueror and warrior. At times, he was confused of what reality meant, like a stranger wandering in the desert and stricken by the singe of the sun, only his subsistence, saved by oasis. The mystery of his philosophies kept coming fearlessly. Who can even advise him of what leads to longevity? When one meets a need, a propelling force diminishes the effort to keep the load, in this; a new energy is sought. Tania developed tumor at the section of the uterus and gave up the ghost. There was a post mortem examination and an autopsy report issued by a Pathologist, who stated, she suffered urethritis of the urethra. She had a taste of her own medicine so to say by her critics. On hearing her untimely demise, Animal was devastated. His heart grieved and disheartened by her departure from him. He rushed to the scene and felt her body, which was cold and showed no sign of life, then burst into tears. He struck matches to light the tobacco. Placing the pipe to his mouth, he smoked and blew out a stream of smoke to his grieving and sober heart, bringing a gist of warmth in his voice. A classic funeral arrangement quickly took place. Placed in a coffin with her engraved name, hearse carried her body to the funeral ground. Sightseers hovered around her body before cremated in a casket, to catch a glimpse of her asymmetric face. Her corpse appeared lovely and her mouth exposed her incisors, canine teeth, and molars, as if laughing. Lying in state, she looked more beautiful than when alive. A headstone and cremains held in the urn, kept in her house afterward. The funeral consumed the day with a wakeful night. Hearing the news Tania had gone to meet her Maker, Animal's Officials gathered to visit him, a time to warm the cockles of his heart; happy their so-called affectionate relationship will be no more. They saw it as a fate ordained death, as one who incurred the wrath of iniquity. Her death gave them the strength to criticize her. Deathswallowed its own. When her deed is put to test, fire will find her out to either heaven or hell. Nothing hidden escapes the presence of her Maker. Perceiving that her bereavement might annul Animal's misery, knowing he wanted her out of the way if ever with the slightest chance; his Officials made provisions for alcoholic beverages for jubilation. They went ensemble to see him in high-spirit, arriving only to discern bizarre atmosphere. They drew to him with heavy hearts. It actually turned out to be an inconsolable sadness. He was crying. For him to appreciate they were concerned, all stood beside him to help him cry, even went further weeping and wailing. Men of dignity, forced to cry like babies. An attendant came with a cup to fetch the drop of tears, and afterward dried their eyes. As a mark of honor, six minutes silence then earmarked for the daughter of the stars. Animal paid tribute to his deceased wife with a mournful song, a dirge:I will always love you as much as I can. The candle burnt away to shut her eyes. I cannot help it out of sight to my last breath.

Love has eaten into me, to the heart's abode.

The cloud cries, overwhelmed with passion.

Who opened the door to the dead when not invited?

Death gazed at the corner to enlist his army.

He comes like a friend, but I knew him not. He knew me, but I tore myself from him. No one ever wished to die when not his time.

A companion for life tasted death's sour tongue.

Nothing can fill the vacuum for soul blown apart.

The surging sea mounted up, the waves swelled.

Why cry in a time of euphoria? Why laugh in a time of mourning?

Death took the place of attainment when issues still unfold.

Think it over, only if worthwhile.

Surely not worth a try, when it makes no sense.

I proclaim what is evident, for enquiries see the wind.

She left to the land of the dead, where silence lives.

She went the way of all flesh, to return to earth no more.

The bell of a trumpet called in the middle of the City.

O! That she may enter the doors of the womb, consoled once more in conception. Stillness in the voice, only heard in dreams. The leaves withered, Hero of the piece fell from the tree.

She held her nobility in high esteem. Dignified silence is exactly where she belongs.

Graveyard is insensitive to death's pain, when taken alone in the dead of night. Malevolence, with malice aforethought chose the underworld and the ways of the dead.

Much kisses from me, from the perfumes' mouth. The kiss of life comes once in a lifetime.

Ah, who knows if the dead shares mere tears? The answer is only for great men to know.

She left at a time to need me most. The fact remains that death has no friend. Never wish for death, he is not kind. For the dead of death resides in eyes of Chamber.

If death, which came into being due to disobedience, had been swallowed in the lake of fire and no more, we would have lived forever. He was not there for her when she needed his attention. Casians are great celebrators of their dead. Myths of supernatural powers were held in high esteem. The dead are known to reincarnate which appeared absurd, to the known fact of hell and heaven. Onlydemons imitate the features of the dead, and choose to materialize to mortals on earth. Rulers who led a fulfilling life and admired by the masses were granted honorary obsequies. In the case of a male, he was not buried alone if he ever had wife or wives. They lined up in a file. If an incantation during the time of cryonics led to the dead sneezing, talking, or smiling, won't he, buried alone, signify he is alive? Floral decorations were sent to the graveyard on most occasions to pay homage. Those imagined as cruel and hated where not giving a peaceful and befitting burial, but had an isolated burial site. One might wonder why so much spent on funeral to the departed when dead than alive. Animal was struck bedridden almost for four days to mourn his dead. In spite of this, he is not at all a celibate for a reclusive life. His nerve itching fidgety could not push him into an era of occlusion to obstruct his field of vision. Henceforth, he began to play thefield. On the sixth day, he felt empty and ordered a virgin to attend to him. He made love to her. The string of her hymen was torn. His Officials heard the scream of an unripe fruit calling out for her Mother. It is demeaning when a man takes advantage of a woman without marrying her. Keeping one's dignity as a virgin first and foremost accords respect by a husband to his wife. Then his face took a lovely and angelic smile when consoled, normally seen when he had a lot of money.

Driven by the impetus for procurement of highly sophisticated weapons of mass destruction, ammunition, and nuclear warheads launched with mobiles and remote controls, every mining site for minerals after excavation modified into research laboratories underground. The Casians had in possession tanks, anti-tank missiles, fleet of supersonic high tech jet fighters fastest in miles per hour and to an altitude high in feet at high performance. Moreover, chemical, nuclear and biological weapons were at their laboratories. Because they were anxious about possible invasion, artillery of all kinds were positioned at critical points and had also woven detonating bombs on the ground unnoticed at a far distance covering the forest zones and vantage areas to the laboratory to inflict physical pain. The slightest attempt to step on will trigger a blast. They were burnt on devising wicked acts. A large throng of combat troops with watchful eyes always twisted their heads to show signs of suspicion and mostly frowned which looked very weird. They got their funds from trafficking illicit drugs like opium, heroin, cocaine,morphine, hemp, hashish, and cannabis to different countries with their submarine. The submarine was also used to explore the bed of the sea for scientific purpose and ancient treasure hunt. As a Drug Lord, he ensured shipment and plantation was on course. Vast arable land was available for cultivation of these drugs in addition to other plants of the same kind in leaves. On reaching their destinations, the drugs permeate the market and filter through the business of buyers. Not only drug trafficking, but smoking as well, which posed dangerous and pernicious to human health. Addiction and drug abuse were killing them softly without their notice. Smoking tobacco, to breathe in chemicals and gases, and drugs infused into the veins were gradually lenient to them now, but exposing them to premature death because of lung cancer that damages the cilia of the lungs, and also reveal stroke, migraine, ulcers, and heart diseases with severe narcotic effect. It brings a feeling of euphoria, hallucinations, paranoia, and restlessness when hooked on drugs, as one accounted an incident of seeing goats and foxes flying like birds in the galaxies, and porcupines chasing the wind as they wafted through the air. Another as well, complained of seeing himself standing on his head balanced upside down, and talking from the eyes. As they indulged in hard drugs, they smoked themselves into an early grave. Whatever medium to abuse drugs leaves an entire damage to the body. Animal had a hand in this operation. If he had been a real animal, his bloodthirsty drive would have gripped its prey by the claws before devouring. There was also a market place trading adultery and prostitution, where demand even exceeded supply. Most Sex Workers are into this job only because they lack money and descent jobs. Animal manipulated people, and tried to bend them to his will. Citizens were obliged to pay excessive tax imposed with the aim to have their children enlisted into his movement, trained for warfare and as hardcore child soldiers, knowing that they will default payments. Non-compliance paved the way for grave annihilation. His own people lived in seclusion and bondage. Honestly, Animal faced an angry backlash from the Indigenous people over the tax law, wherehe even taxed the dead, for choosing to follow his own course of action, not heeding to advice. He told his combat troops, "Don't be lenient, but deal with them drastically." Swarm of bees and scorpions in a room stung child soldiers who lacked courage and were nervous.

The children learned how to inflict physical pain, to maim aggressively. Strict condition was outlined for them to follow until recognized as a power-working machine to wipe out its challenger, with no humane sense of humor. The dying need to kill was meant to dwell in their minds. How on earth, should children be led into such oppression? The girls and boys had their mouths circumcised, with the intention to groom them, but rather, the sharp pains made them deficient in good sense of sound judgment, morality of worthiness, clemency, and to learn etiquette. On several occasions, these child soldiers watched less dominant animals devoured by lions, taught to hunt wild animals andwatched previous year's executions by the guillotine. This made them obsessed with wickedness to develop a killer instinct. The trainees fought wild animals, had to move heaven with much strength, and to avoid losing than buried alive, they had to fight for their dear lives. Death echoed its inevitable calling to their brains. Mental torture is harmful indeed, and made them entities with incredible cruelty, destructive, with anger fermenting deep inside them. Now had no fear to adopt painful endurance and to mete out inhumane treatment more terrifying, deadly panicky, and traumatic, only to follow orders to commit atrocities, acts of brutality, massacre, and carnage. Bloodbath was a regular routine so tasty to them. Now perfectly eligible for combat service, their power, growth, and strength were now becoming a threat. Animal aimed to captivate their minds at a tender age to give way to torture, paying them well with the proceeds from the drugs. Inthat case, they hardly revolted to instigate rebellion against him, now professionally trained to lead in times of war, and dehumanized to act as combatants, able to build missile defense shields to intercept enemy attacks, a significant thought prefigured as obligatory. Animal and his band of crooks known as the VIPERS soiled their hands and wounded their conscience with deadly machinations, losing moral virtues on being sociable, jovial, friendly, and more conservative, attentive, active, self-confident, dominant and typically tolerant. There was an instance to ground helicopter entering Casa City's territory. Unfortunately, the Pilot never got to his country again. Animal's absolute dominion was to rule with iron hands,unquestionable behavior as a sign of superiority, with an invariable disposition, prone to destruction.

However, he was soon to face fierce backlash from his adversaries. Someone devised rebellion to assassinate Him. The bond of fealty damaged along the line, as an Official of his conspired against him.

Dorbi knew the ordeal his wife went through, but on deception that, she was at home when cruelly murdered. All along, he had the notion Animal carried the order that was erroneously Tania, when she murdered the woman in the Grave

Garden. Who will ever accept as true, this fabrication? When informed, on that faithful day, group of armed men broke into the house and shot her as she lay on the bed. Who knew what transpired in that room before such atrocious act? Dorbi was then on assignment for drug trafficking with his fugitives. He never saw Owusua again until he passed on. Hearing the news of bereavement, Dorbi wept bitterly, vowed to avenge for her death. He was greatly troubled until he saw the settling of scores tasting the terror and horror of the sword. However, if he had figured out the notion that revenge is for the Lord, theworld would have been healthier and peaceful. He deliberated on his wish for vengeance, a conspiracy of silence to topple an oppressive regime. Dorbi started giving Animal a scornful gaze. One can tell a mood of anger in his tone of voice. Annoyance and greed generate sense of alienation, bigotry, bias, inferiority, rejection, and hatred toward others. He knew it would cost him his dear life if anyone tends to divulge to Animal his impending plan. Arrogance and pride took dominion to a callous crave for devastation. In this, he lacked the quality to conceal a murderous face. Violating the vow of allegiance and trust that severed will put his life in the line of fire. His eyes strained with longing for quick relief as the need to sleep always flee from his eyes. His mind will not be at rest until pacified.

His facial expression drew much concern and worry as he lingered on a figment of imagination as though one worn out of hunger. This anticipation to kill brought a path of ruin instead of unity; settling of scores instead of harmony, apathy instead of love, and backbiting instead of unity. The greedy appetite for retaliation eats the brains awkwardly until carried out. Legitimacy to the brevity of humanity is to soften our hearts and advocate for civility in discourse. Discarding an argument to irritate anger and suppressing a quarrel does not mean you are a coward. It means you have enough sense to save you the trouble of death and injury. This is why we have law and order at work in addition to those destined to defend the Country. Animal was accorded the title of leadership due to his fortune, and when he fearlessly, as a great warrior, wrestled with a lion. He is also a fierce wrestler. Anyone who challenged his leadership had to wrestle with him for supremacy, which is in direct contrast to a democratically elected government as Indigenous people decide on their leaders. This ceased to exist after Salt City took over Casa City.

One day, Dorbi called on a servant of Animal. He told her, "Can I trust you?" She answered, "Sure of course, why not, even to the limit of having your fat head in my juicy throat." He spoke to her, "Okay, have this venom of a serpent, eh. I will like you to accomplish this task on my behalf. I think Animal is truly sick in the head, and to euthanize him will definitely fit him. Just mix it with Animal's tea and serve him with it, even a little will end him, honestly, just a little will do, and then you will have a handsome reward. They parted company, only to get in touch with a wait and see stand to find out the outcome.

When the servant appeared before Animal to serve him tea from a flask into a cup, she revealed the assassination attempt to him. Animal construed he was in an internal power struggle. He promoted her to tidy his bedroom every day, in addition to money reward. Animal organized a party, calling all his Officials. He ordered his servant to mix the venom with Dorbi's drink, besides, the best of his food for him to eat his last meal on this planet. In his opinion, Dorbi is fit to join his ancestors. The gate to the dead wants followers in his premises. Any threat to his unique identity as a person called for elimination. The party was wild, sexy, and hot. Singing and dancing lit the place. Animal assigned beautiful women to him, taken over his attention. Dorbi was caught unaware of what lies ahead. A Colleague tried to signal to him for the danger beforehand with a frown of condemnation, but he was lost in the snares of illicit women, ensnared, and enslaved to lust. Animal addressed his Officials, "My people, a traitor has betrayed my confidence by fomenting mutiny that sank in dismay. A Rebel among you dared me to a challenge to question my cupidity. The lion loves to feast on elephants, but not grass cutter. "I am not a grass cutter!" Dorbi complained. "Did I mention your name? Oh, so you came here to fight?" Animal asked. "You are not farfrom that assertion," Dorbi answered. "How will that benefit you?" Animal asked. Dorbi exclaimed angrily, "Did you think of that before tasting my wife?" Animal reacted defiantly, "Look at all the women here Dorbi, mature for marriage. The fact that she cheated on you tells of a cuckoo that lays its eggs in other bird's nests. Actually she was an active participant willingly for free. "You should be ashamed of yourself for such an utterance," Dorbi retorted. Animal went on, "A dog does not bite the hand that feeds it. If the frog wants to grow wings to fly, it should ask the bird. When an animal grows horns, it thinks its head is the strongest to gore any challenger. Does the hoe ask the Farmer why handled? He cuts the grass with the sickle for seedlings to grow suitably. Have you ever heeded to anyone answering before a question? Do not hastily call a wrath on yourself, so you can suffer. Let me save you the pain Dorbi. Go and seek fresh blood." He breathed hard, in and outin anger as he exercised his authority over him to ally himself with his command. To underrate an opponent is grievously as bathing hot water on a sunny day. If one could have implemented little restraint, there would not be the need to dig quickly one's early grave. Dorbi also responded furiously with an obvious protest at an act of defiance, "Do not mind this thing trying to be a tsetse fly! Even the least of sheep, I mean the underlings can engage in battle with this son of a vampire; he is throwing dust into our eyes! If it is, the Lords will for the blind being healed, so be it, but know for sure that, the blind man can defeat you. He is a murderer! Let him know surely that the bee is mighty among tigers. He must bear the brunt of cutting back time with my wife in bed. She is no more. I am now alone, and have missed her dearly." Animal despised him as he butted in on him, "Dorbi, you had the nerve to call me a tsetse fly and a vampire? As I see, you want to embrace death. Isn't it?" Dorbi reacted, "Absolutely a soft tsetse fly and a toothless vampire!" Animal retorted, "It seems you lost the way to this place. Just look around for fresh blood. The choice is yours, humble yourself, and ask for forgiveness. Why do you want me to cut out the underworld for you, in so doing, starve yourself of a fitting burial, Dorbi? Are you not better off alive than dead? Why declare your Mother barren? I mean, why! Huh? Have you not heard? Has it never occurred to you that I am capable of bleeding dry your ability and pumping out your aptitude? I feel a deep-seated pity to lash you like one not my own, Dorbi! Stage your case within reach! Lay down your argument shrewdly! Turn now from breaking the rules, reform your deed, and you will once more find your spirit with the living. Why are you seeking for the sword to devour until has lapped up enough blood, in so doing, make me tear you down? You are talking empty words into the air Dorbi. Let the mountains hear what you have to say. Let the wind carry it to the wise, for you are even a dead man before me." Tough provocation and a heated confrontation on either side were awful. Nevertheless, Dorbi trusted his instinct; in no way Animal can ever locate him to a state of repose, never. In a quest to test one's nerve in a fight, let go, stay calm, and pray. Better to act a fool to your opponent, but actually a wise decision, and go your way, than to confront. At least, you save your energy and strength, have enough strength to work for money while testing your potency in bed with your wife, probably keep from premature death. Immediately, both drew their swords. Clash of swords did confirm in the atmosphere. They faced off fiercely as they brandished swords aggressively to deflect affliction, Animal swung at him with the sword to cut his head off. Dorbi suddenly stooped down, bending his head and shoulder forward and slashed below his chest. Luckily, Animal was wearing a metalplate, which he normally did when in action. Dorbi attempted a thrusting movement, but Animal averted the swipe at him, and almost slit his wrist, which he targeted all along, but in a quick attempt, Animal got him. Dorbi abruptly dropped his sword, accepting defeat. Animal was about to run him through, on the contrary, the poison was having effect on him. Dorbi felt feverish with high temperature.

Blood trickled his eyes, mouth and nose, such a tragedy he brought on himself. If Dorbi had not stuck to his guns, he would not have been shattered into pieces. Animal mopped his sword on Dorbi's hair, and then sheathed the sword. The sneer of the adversary is dreaded. Dorbi's face emptied of all color and animation.

No wonder, this awful experience was on account of Animal's past growing up; no affection of a parent for his child, flogged for no reason, mistreated as though, never came from the womb. His stages of development were of no concern to his parents. Animal felt self-conscious when denied parental responsibility. His parents once told him, when they looked at his face and body at birth, he was so tiny, they thought his death would be at an advantage and of assistance to incessant pain, hence they would have aborted his pregnancy with Doctors permission. In that case, it dawned on him; there was a pitiless drift of extreme dislike. This is outrageous! When maltreated, children end up channeling their emotional discomforts and disturbances into wild activities to cause harm to others. The more a child learns weird concept, the likelihood to grow up with perception influenced to depict ethical decay. When it suggests itself that one is shorn of basic source of living, and hardship becomes a daily work, insurgency, sexual immorality, and crime are scarcely ruled out. At an immature age, children are more vulnerable to be ledastray by peer group. Neglected children and others born out of wedlock, with lack of proper discretion mostly account for juvenile delinquency. Children stray from the path of good moral upbringing when no parental control holds them in check. A naughty way of life only creates route to destruction, thereby heaping coals on the head. When parents keep stern watch over their children, it is difficult for peer pressure to influence them. Society is suppose to create the enabling environment for expression of views, giving attention to each individual whose innate self being corrupted with unavoidable vice, to be on familiar terms with the senses to live. If not, that is a nightmare when the forces of nature must require answers from the spiritual realm to think through the mind of humanity. Parents must have much insight to bear the liability for shaping children's development, introspection, and curious precocity. Children all the time want to have their own way. It is up to Parents, with love, kindness, and care, explain the outcome of what they crave for, just to stay out of anything to cause trouble. For instance, the most effective way for a Teacher to teach a student is to assume the role of a student to identify weakness and strength, then, the Teacher can appreciate the tendency to teach with the heart and mind, but not only the mind. When a child attains puberty, he or she questions the looks of the body's features when experiencing physical and psychological changes, then intends to stress much on independence, distinctiveness, and individuality. After completing school, there comes the onus to look for job. The desire to settle down and have a family is well thought out. At growth, choices might lead to midlife crisis or recovery to life fulfillment, before approaching retirement and old age. Life ceases to exist when the eyes are shut. As the saying goes, "You are only youngonce." God entrusted parents with the responsibility not to lead children astray and wayward, but to care for them completely. If any child loses the way of light, God will demand their soul from the parents. Likewise, anyone trying to take on a leadership role or management position should uncover past performance and prior record of accomplishment obvious to the masses. Beneath Animal's deep soul was one who wanted to kill his fear that engulfed him, which actually generated the atmosphere to crush anyone being of hindrance. Notwithstanding, good deeds can find abode among scoundrels. It is never in vain to come on this earth.

4. MEDICAL CREW

The ship dispatched to patrol the coast as it drifted out to sea was almost nearing Casa City, going on a fact-finding mission to carry their intensive search with rapt attention and try to siphon a bank of information, pinpointing definite and concrete tracking routes. The Crew was also team of researchers with the formidable task to develop, test and make available drugs as antidotes suitable in checking all deadly diseases, and to ensure more safer and effective environment. Already informed of the fact on ground, it beckoned on the Crew to act with much insight into gathering information with extensive intelligence, stemming from thefact that their lives were at risk, on the greatest dread of their safety if they tried to play things down. The Crew had with them communication gadgets and hidden cameras as part of their medical equipment. A snap of photo from the camera immediately registers the picture at the Intelligence Service laboratory. As they went through the normal routine at the coast of Casa City, their presence seemed acceptable to the Guards and were allowed to carry on their work, but with strict vigilance. The next day, the Crew was at work to dole out quality health care to the people. Once a while, they could notice that, angry and contemptuous looks were cast on them from every angle. This forced them to raise tempest of persuasive laughter or smile when a VIPER came close to them, which often confused the VIPERS with absurd misunderstanding of this Crew laughing. Citizens were vaccinated and the medical team was always available at the wards.

Throng of children trooped in their numbers for inoculation, accompanied by their parents, especially mothers, a defense mechanism immune to attacks. They were advised on all that it takes to live a healthy life, on a healthy diet, with all the nutrients and vitamins with vitality recommended for healthy living, and to also accommodate a clean lifestyle. Their presence was beneficial to the Citizens. The Medical Crew also took it upon themselves to visit the Indigenous people at their respective houses, observing their conditions, in addition to their surveillance project. Although not struck dumb, the monitoring team was saddened by the awkward treatment. Nevertheless, they knew their passion would win the day. It occurred to them the Citizens of Casa City were left without happiness, love, affection, and handicapped by isolation with no redress of grievances. The plight of the people drew the Medical Team with empathy.

There was a mist formation in the cloud, darkened in thick fog in the morning, but at dusk, it lifted. Niksi, one of the medical team was very alert and had the chance to have a look around to grasp the nub of the situation. He had fine sideburns and side whiskers.

He put on a mask at midnight, and costumed like the VIPERS, he dived underneath the sea, got to a narrow tunnel with bars secured with locks, locked with padlocks. Probably an escape route in time of danger, leading to the Castle where Animal was. So he returned to his colleagues. The following night, he got tools ready and attempted again. He had access in and swam through a canal with very clean water, to a space leading to the alley and the yard. He managed to swerve VIPERS at post and entered a pathway that led to a loft connected to the ceiling, until he arrived at a place where a meeting was ongoing,mindful of concealed video cameras that scanned everywhere. Heeavesdropped on them, listening with rapt attention, and then snapped photos of the group. He wired the place for feedback by placing a communication device and a recorder there to transmit information to his colleagues and the Intelligence laboratory, who listened in on what transpired. Anytime a meeting is to convene, his Officials keep standing, beat their chest proudly to welcome Animal. He walks with diligence to his seat, sits down, and then his Officials do the same, sitting next to each other with swords beside them. Animal talked with a clear huge voice, "We have to test our missiles and soon to prepare launching, in that case, I want your suggestions on a point of direction, to allow me quench my inner drive, without a notice of its source. Then to jubilate on its impact and the disastrous blow it will cause. "The acquisition of knowledge corrupted with coercive retaliation. Animal drew on his pipe, and then went on, "We have to take this Medical Team very seriously. The Citizens crave a sight of them, and love clinging to them as if a baby and it's Mother. These men and women are spies, look; their faces even attest that fact clearly, without a doubt, and can even smell it on them, testifying to the urge to poke around with eyes in their mouths. I have no doubt they have skeletons in their closets. We have to rummage through their lodging house to figure out what they are up to before they got any hint of what is to come. Immediately they finish their assignments, there will be bloodshed for a birthday. Those in full agreement should say I, and those against should say no." He slammed his fist on the table in rage. His Officials responded, "Yeah!" They lifted glasses and drank a toast. All this while, Animal had a sneaking suspicion as he twisted his head around. Niksi wanted to make a bold attempt at them but left them to the Special Forces, also known as Combat Contingent, who will soon deal with them.

He spoke to himself, "How can you strike alliance with a mad man of a recalcitrant nature hard to please, with no solid profile? The next time, he will amend his ways and manners and behave politely. He will put an end to the cruel manners and such outrageous insults to our dignity. For sadness is not always the owner of defeat." In a breathless hush to leave that place, he raised his eyebrows to denote surprise at that auspicious moment. Startling awareness actually led his conscience to conduct his search with such haste and attentiveness. He knew the tragic moment would be awfully nice if caught, which was a likely calculated attempt on his dear life to pass away. Why kick the bucket when not yet finished enjoying his wife? He cannot afford his manhood cut off with a chain saw. After all a tree has a life in it. He would have been of no use to his wife. Niksi began to cast backward glance propelled by forward momentum of impact and the likely risk ahead as he buried his head in his palms and attempted to check on the Medical Crew right away. He ensured of feedback as he bugged their conversation with listening and surveillance device with hidden microphone. Before leaving, a robotic device, very small, with video camera took a stage in the Castle, easing the tedious work to parachute it or use drones to maneuver to its destination.

Trying to sneak out of a door to exit, he entered a large room, one of brilliance of architecture. He yawned loudly, which caught the attention of lioness with her cubs lying inactive. Definitely, he will make their day. Casa City had lions on guard as well. It never crossed his mind to encounter such a scene. Ravenous lions that would not spare him interrupted his movement. He had to unearth his potential, shield himself from the unexpected, to work his way out unharmed. Forced to ginger a simple-minded initiative to his incisivereminiscence, looking at the next line of action, the lions were now playing psychological imaginations on their opponent to see if scared, roared, a sign of pre-eminence. He has to get out. He made a dash for the door with such an impatient glance, and had to open the door for his escape. He stood at the door fumbling with the key already in place. The door had code provided you can key in the password, as well as the use of bunch of keys. Tired and frustrated as his hands shook a little, he made an advanced attempt and the door swung open. Immediately, a wave of anticipation and expectation swept through him. The lions were furious and attempted to pounce on him. His leg entangled on a rope and he fell. He had a smoke grenade with him, which was mostly used by Special Forces for combat operations, and released it to impede their vision and to suffocate the lions. He opened the door locked it behind, and heaved a sigh of relief. His bundle of joy drew smile on his face, but watchful as well. The door led to a room with a programmed chair that when you sit on and code in figures, you descend to a cave leading to a research library and the underground rail line. If he can make it to the medical crew, the only place to pass had VIPERS stationed on the lookout. He broke through them, slide out of view, and fortunately made it safely to his colleagues. He knew if caught, the VIPERS would have taken him as dead animal protein tossed to hyenas. Informed of the asteroid, he later recognized the place was heavily guarded. After narrating everything to the Crew, they quickly hid all the sophisticated gadgets.

Animal started developing interest in Monica, one of the Medical Scientists. Her dressing found her out as she was always exposing more than required. Who dare withstand such enticement, the lure of enchantment? It takes a strong-minded spirit to overcome. Directed by lust, Animal became besotted with her. God in his infinite understanding had his handiwork appearing gorgeous. Phantasm took over. She won his affection. He extended a holistic approach to enhance the appealing mood, providing the ultimate recipe to get on with her, or derive a unique modus operandi to calm his state of mind, an attempt to know her intimately to recognize her flaws. He worked out his amatory advancement proficiently. It is worth a try to tell her his impression of her. He sends her flowers and kindhearted words, making every attempt for her to notice his interest, and provided her the access to move freely. He itched to sleep with her. Then the medical crew stipulated on the need to capitalize on that to nail him down. One early morning, their door flung open, sounding like sparking a car, and VIPERS trooped in. As they shoved into the room, Animal followed and stood before them. He cleared his throat and voiced out authoritatively, "Monica, come with me now!" Women do not take such style of advancement lightly. They want to experience that affectionate and caring tactics to depict fondness. She hesitated, almost fearful of appending threat and knew she might involve herself in an act against her will. Why follow somebody who has lost his line of reasoning, with a recondite fit of pique? She took him as one who was not quite right in the head, where she does not know how long he might get back the use of his senses precisely, a psychosis of insanity in his own world. However, Animal wanted to have a child with her by any means possible in his power as the leader. Observing her reluctant impression, he shouted, "It is a command, now!" A wave of paranoia surged painfully through her. She followed them and they drove away. The medical team troubled of the possible outcome. Arriving at the castle, they climbed the stairs and went through a door to a spacious living room decorated and well furnished with pictures pasted to the walls. He showed her hidden rooms, but not all. Later, they drove off to meet the combat troops. Monica was terrified but pretended things were moving on smoothly. She saw bombs and artillery of all kinds at a laboratory, promoting several scientific expeditions, exploration and research, the hard training of VIPERS running and engaging in jungle warfare, tedious exercises, how to lay traps and ambush in forest zones, wrestling with wild animals, and dog training. She also saw how the dogs were trained to lead in battle, able to attack, causing assault just like their combat troops. She noticed how the VIPERS honed their brains to remain alert and focused. Looking a bit scared, Monica had to catch her breathing level that speeded her heartbeat, on numerous of times to keep her alive. If she had been the mother, she would have presumed an advisory role to a child to pump sense into his unyielding brain, disciplined in the teachings of Holy Books. What you cultivate in a child leads to maturity. If you plant garden eggs, you reap garden eggs, and if you grow mangoes, you harvest mangoes. That is the rule of nature. Turning blind eyes to its magnitude that grinds on reality cannot leave behind principles of nature, but highly, to be ahead of continuous modern trends. Later, they returned to the castle. Animal knew Monica is not fully acquainted with her. He suspected she was a woman of questionable character. She wished to be superior in all things and control him, which was never possible in Animal's terrain of jurisdiction. She was self-centered, and he has to determine what sort of person she is, struggling to build an intimate love relationship with her. He took her around to draw a sign of superiority, his power, and strength, difficult to bow down to pressure and willnever accept defeat. However, she looked quite tensed and nervous with watchful eyes, which was one of annoyance and slight displeasure, and then dissolved into a mask of sorrow and grief. Completely empty of emotions, she wished to teach him a lesson that will never escape his mind if she had the power, to turn his unhelpful mind around, and will remember once more sucking his mother's breast when a baby, or perhaps having wet dreams. Deep within, she lashed insults at him. However, she took advantage of her beauty to gather much information to the Combat Contingent. After bathing, he ordered her to do the same. In the course of bathing, she douched clean, and then went to the living room. Animal sat beside her and leaned over to kiss her cheek with passionate love. His piercing eyes caught her cleavage with thin beautiful line of the alphabet, "I." He could not withstand the arduous wish for righteousness, to remain pure and untainted, as strong feeling of affection for such coitus mood led to an undivided attention, clearly to have her in the buff. His mouth smelled of peppermint. He offered her a drink. As they watched television, Animal started playing with her breasts, performing exploits on her body as he squeezed so affectionately. She tried to pull away but he grabbed her firmly, then delicately with a smile. "What is it now? What do you think you are doing?" She raised a curious voice. He responded, "Come on darling, don't waste much time, you know what I mean." Luring, he won't take no for an answer. She shrugged her shoulders and murmured defiantly. "What do you mean?" She asked. He assured, "Take it easy, you will be fine." His persuasive intent had an effect as he went on fondling. She was turned on. Her breasts stood firm and rigid as her sternum enlarged. Her heart leapt from its place. Monica felt uneasy, and unnerving, with a look of surprise, obviously, her hair stood on end. She tried to resist, but was horrified of her safety and life. How can she give in to a stranger she found objectionable? She knew what he was up to all this while, with no doubt to rule her vulnerability. You feel endless drive for each other when there is common understanding. He caressed her softly and got her in the vibes of arousal, and then sucked her bazoom. Moving his hand down under her skirt, she hesitated, but was so weak to fight back as she was now yearning for more. He slipped her zip open to catch a glimpse of her. Now feeling refreshed, alert and his conscience cleared of heavy loads, he signaled his head to assure of complete comprehension. His penetrating eyes liked what he saw. There was an air of quiet competence. He made gestures of entreaties, trying to delve into her mind as he looked on intently, but here she was, ensnared in a moment of fantasy. Hardly to wait for the endless desire burning within her, he quickly undressed and kissed her. He was hard on, stiff, and big. He was ready to fight the battle with well-endowed education. She opened the lips of her minge to welcome him. He began to penetrate her with care. She felt the friction in the form of rubbing the two hands together. She moaned, sharing tears as she fumbled, "It hurts, but keep on, you are almost there." He then thrust in and out, and increased the speed. Her melodious voice softened like tasting something juicy. Another thrust, ouch, taking her breath to a different realm. She heard him say, "I love you." Her mouth was quivering and it burnt hot inside, like oven, fully aware of the thickness and capacity to have him in her. Feelings of erotic consciousness were building within. He was now at the peak of his career and he experienced some succulent thirst-quenching sensation cropping in, an intense libido, mind blowing, he couldn't help it, and…ouch…ash! O Lord Almighty!

The source of our strength…He ejaculated with her. He liked how her pubic hair shaved in style, exposing her loins bare with an inscription of a key. Temptation pierced his heart, and he could not resist her beauty, taking a glance of her face that illustrated one of innocence. She aroused and quenched his appetite.

Looking at him straight in the eye to have a face-to-face talk, "You were excellent." Making her losing her virginity excited him, as his heart was very calm. She studied him thoughtfully and patiently, trying to sort out everything in his mind. He had a genuine liking for her, as he gave her a huge grin, a very infectious smile. He whispered in her ears, "How often will you like me to carry on?" Ah, this is a hectic time to ask that question. Can't you see she is trying to catch her breath? Can't you remember? The proof of the pudding is in the eating. Her breathing speeded as her heart was beating hard. However, she answered, "Please continue on countless times, but take your time." His obsession with her had given a rough ride. His fingers were perfectly at work, critically touring her sensitive organs and erogenous zones with tidy surrounding to find her G-Spot, making exploits delicately with tender care to fathom the beauty of femininity until he reawakened his potency. This time, he moved his body to the rhythm, with much tenderness, striking too deep to her uterus, focusing on hitting the spot she felt deep excitement. She screamed, another thrust and...oops! She gasped and sobbed hysterically, a gush of tingling elation as hot as she murmured, "Sh...ash... please." A creamy wetness, like thick liquid similar to what she normally discharged in between her legs monthly built in her, as if they swam into perfect abode. She wept within, mixed with pain and full sugary, and he gave her a kiss on her clear loins. The waves sparkled. He really made her day. Both slept to simmer down.

When she woke up, Animal pretendedasleep, but tilted his eyelid a bit open, dropped his eyelash in the form of blinking, to observe her movement. With carefully calculated footstep, Monica aimed at the door, and then her heart flew from its place when Animal changed his posture on the bed. She thought he was awake, only to demand for more fun, but came to realization, it was not. She can't stand much more of him. She never had Animal at heart, but enjoyed the moment they just experienced. Monica quickly walked out almost naked, running for her dear life when not pursued, as if she left her brains at home. Even horses do not gallop as such. Animal burst into laughter. He got what he loved most, tasting forbidden fruit, which under normal circumstance given customarily, by meeting the demands of the female's parents. Perhaps, he deserves the amiable time with her. After all, his position gratifies him the power to satisfy his sexual ego, and cannot withstand self-control.

Taking care of all his children with the numerous concubines give him headache. The guards outside saw her and jeered at her. Monica made it safely to the medical crew. They demanded her to spill the beans when asked what happened. She responded, "He slept with me." They chastised her, "He slept with you just like that? Where was your sense of reason? How possible?" She questioned, "Are you trying to insult me? They replied, "Not at all, we only expected you of all people to know better. Did you like it?" She replied, "Don't you know where we are? I was scared to be on death row. It was within his power to have what he wanted. You know well we are in a lion's den. He entered into me andpossessed me." The Crew reassured her to keep the pretense of loving to sleep with him to inform on him. She seethed quietly into her room, straightened her shaggy hair, washed with lavender oil, and then rinsed it thoroughly. The medical crew was more watchful andcareful in their ways. With the urge to pay attention, they could inhale victory in the air, to obstruct them from going astray, and making shipwreck of their lives, keeping their brains renewed and purified like the snake, that creeps in gradually, without the realization of its prey. All along, vigilance never escaped their eyes to give clear-cut information to enable paratroopers easily invade, scheming with precision and simply drop supplies, ammunitions and vehicles able to be dismantled and assembled quickly. Nonetheless, no one has ever left alive in that territory. Even the life of the Medical Crew was really at stake; hope to leave with burden carried in the head.

5. MISSION

Counting on the President's words, the Military, Immigration, Police, Prisons, Fire Service, and INTERPOL, were prepared to take action, fully alert for the mission. Calling for active involvement, troops were swiftly mobilized to contend with the VIPERS, girding their loins for the task ahead. This led to the demand for Special Forces, chosen to complete the mission on schedule, and assumed the names, TORNADO, EAGLES, and COBRAS or FALCONS. Without a speck of doubt, dexterity in marksmanship guaranteed firing with precision and barely missing the mark, in addition, to outline milieu of routes to strike in Casa City. With their faces like ascorching furnace, these men and women of value fought valiantly, those you could vouch for in their duties, to what we call, Indefatigable Fighters, and Salt City's finest. There was premedication to enhance their operations. The root of the issue is of life and death. If they cannot do it on time, war is then declared. Nevertheless, the result will be unbearable. It will be a devastating blow to their safety, because, Casa City was fully prepared for unforeseen contingencies. The VIPERS can only be defeated by making out grit of resilience, toughness, and limitations peculiar to them. In spite of this, there is still an undefeated record of accomplishment, where previous interventions led to no scrap of trace to where they came from. On parade ground, Soldiers marched to melodious songs in an echelon formation and arrow head. Those in front and rear threw and caught batons, then a spin of batons. "Halt!" the order went. "Attention! Wiggle your waist! Atease! That's right. Mark time!" The stamp of feet went with compliance to order. The Special Forces lined up while marching to fall in and stood rigidly and confidently, snapped to attention and saluted with full control of their bodies. Afterward, they exchanged cordial greetings, and then stood at ease. There was gun salute for the martyrs of the land. To the Military, death is an honour not left to any chance, but on bravery and bold heart of a lion. Sampson addressed them, shouting and walking up and down in front of them. He yawned, and immediately he opened his mouth, it twisted his talking, making it blurred and unclear. He said sorry and continued speaking. His lips curved into a smile, and then quickly spoke in an angry condescending voice with the gravity of his words strictly harsh, " We are men of stature and have to unravel the mystery, so

I kindly urge you to prepare for the task ahead, to deal aggressively with the VIPERS what they deserve for such awful vileness. Our mission is to rescue our own and sneak out unnoticed, and with all assurance, have Animal rather executed, for if the lion sleeps, the lamb will play. We are going out there to intercept the very personification of evil, and the vicious cycle of malice, aware of embarking on a dangerous mission. We are fully mindful of the outcome. Military advancement will normally take place before dawn if necessary to aid operation. Our main focus is to capture the trouble maker, that notorious ruffian, making it easier to release the T.B.A. in prison, and now calling for liberation of our own, by adopting more intellectual approach, to ensure we impede the invasion of VIPERS, and we are more than ever determined to take Casa City over." He spoke with abrupt dexterity, boosting their self-esteem, an archetype of a warrior and an architect of a conqueror, spelling out his intention and instruction clearly. An air of confidence kindled their courage for an aggressiveincursion into Guerrilla strongholds. They fell out after session. The Combat Contingent was specially trained Officers, mighty Forces to be reckoned with. Their works cut across putting forward new techniques to unravel all hidden agenda, to look out for a mine of information, both within and out of the country, and were fully equipped for the task. These men and women endured strenuous military exercises to enhance mental alertness, strengthened their muscles to improve stamina and physical fitness with keen military antennae as physical and mental endurance were put to test. Illustrating the assignment to them, the TORNADO'S believed in the omen of one always prepared for inexorable eventuality of life, an ability to take a calculated risk on catastrophe, and turbulence. They are seen as those raised outside sentiments, especially at the level of education to have a virtue of necessity, fully aware of evil that sporadically continued everywhere inCasa City. They stipulated clear-cut military formation in divisions, with anti-aircraft and missile defense shields in position at vantage points, and first aid provision during an injury, had in possession a map with apt description and specific direction, with military logistics for operation,supplies, moving equipment and missile guidance systems with launcher. Surface-to-surface, air-to-air, and surface-to-air missiles were also mounted. The President gave a seal of approval for deployment. A unit will survey proceedings and when clear, the next unit will parachute to the Castle to capture Animal, with additional unit to launch massive attack and charge on the VIPERS, before the prisoners' arrival at the execution site, all to happen at same time. The Military advanced in organized formation with large contingent of troops, clear-headed and ready for combat. Aggression was intensifying. Salt City's submarine now stationed precisely inplace, keeping track of radar signals. Asidegallant Armed Forces, highly mechanized equipment for surveillance, drones, murderous accompanying aircrafts, and Archers were all positioned considerably in place, a distance away from Casa City, kept unnoticed by Animal and his VIPERS In case of inexorable circumstance, there is no option than to discharge huge casualties on the VIPERS. The FALCONS, TORNADO, and EAGLES also had in possession bows and arrows, crossbows and bolts, to shoot where silence finds abode and ought to swallow the sound of the gun. They also intended to target all areas that may be useful to the enemy; their source of funding, and where their weapons are kept. The shepherd's duty is to protect vulnerable sheep falling victim to wild animals. The Divisions of Expeditionary Forces packed their bags and baggage from the barracks, bid farewell to their respective families who kept watching during departure, and headed to the Air Force base with their trained dogs.

Determination leads to perseverance with the utmost drive to impel risking it all with maximum effort, for in confidence lies boldness and vice versa, courage to withstand insurmountable condition, and as usual, always sticking to principles. Dangerous missions demand fearless, daring, courageous, spirited, and brave men, advancing to treacherous territories under the cover of darkness with their eyes to light their sights. The President urged them to stay safe and wished them luck.

High performance jets with high speed and high altitude flights were ready for the FALCONS, TORNADO, and EAGLES. The Pilots in quick succession did safety checks on these airplanes. With seat belts fastened and helmets on, these Pilots set in motion the switches, inserted the keys into the ignitions in the ceiling to start the engines. For a Pilot to fly the plane, he or she keeps to complex course of action, like checking all control buttons in the cockpit, including the transponder. The plane strolls across to taxi, and with the steering wheel, steers the plane to hit the runway. The Mobile Unit signals a green light. The Pilot speaks to the Controller until cleared to take-off. Pilots are informed of airworthiness by radio from the air traffic control. The Pilot adds power and steps on the rudder pedals. Like greased lightning, the plane speedily lifts into the air, after arriving at enough speed, streaking across the sky confidently and majestically, climbing until hidden in the sky and soundless, not scared perhaps of any injury when Experts are skillfully in charge. Now, the Crew listened earnestly as the plane reached its destination, a calculated distance, nearer to Casa City. The Combat Contingent heaved their parachutes over their backs and flew out of the plane with their dogs. In mid-air, they pulled their ripcords and landed safe and sound in the forest and near the Medical Crew, very careful of hidden traps, and immediately fixed their sophisticated gadgets to start intelligence gathering, gallantly ready for battle. The TORNADO aligned themselves with the mission in a well-organized formation, made certain nothing span out of hand, and took into consideration civilian casualties. There was a Cartographer with them to delineate specific route to VIPER terrain, well thought-out of any armed resistance. Inconspicuous camouflage disguised their visibility, hardly recognizable, wearing coat of armor and bandolier, a protective vest, uniform with helmets, a costume designed to save from harm, the very delicate parts of the body. When the need arises, they have to wear the uniforms as that of the VIPERS they kill. As they cut their way through the thick forest, the TORNADO sought to acquire information from anybody found in the forest, a vital component to the assignment, while the dogs moved about to divulge any unseen trap. Where needed, they trekked in a lineup. Luckily, a hunter was seen trekking in the forest, armed with guns, sword, bow and arrows. The Combat Contingent moved toward him, spoke kindly to him, however, would have used force if reluctant to cooperate. They were aware most hunters led strangers to the VIPERS by trying to be nice to them. He provided all information he knew about Casa City, orchestrating every detail. However, was circumspect about how dicey they were to danger. Initially, he pondered over telling the truth or not. He took into consideration his life being at stake as a traitor, if recognized leaking information. To ensure that was perhaps, a pervasion of reality, the Combat Contingent demanded aggressively his name and children; this was verified with the Medical Crew. Anyone seen with intruders encroaching Guerrilla or Militant domain was killed.

The Medical Crew confirmed for accurate information. The hunter had his reward, but told with stern caution, "We wouldhave done justice to you, by cutting your wife's delicacy, that she enjoyed to get pregnant, if you had lied to us." Apparently, he knew the City well, but was enticed with money to provide the needed information to explore every nook and cranny. His prolonged talk, with endearing tenderness in his voice consumed precious time, as his heart was in a logical dispensation, as well, was not sure if his life protected out of danger. The Special Forces patted his shoulder to assure him of protection, but would have to stay with them. Vigilance never escapes the sight of an eagle. When mentally alert, as they aimed assiduously to their destinations, they advanced to the center of the City. The driving force intensified. The trees also aided their surveillance as they watched hidden in the leaves and branches in the day and night while heedful of the terrors of darkness, the beasts of the forest, so called nocturnal predators. At dusk, theHunter planned to chop sticks for firewood.

Duri queried his behaviour as if she owned him, "What do you think you are doing?" "It's getting dark and we have to light fire." The Hunter answered, as he felt cold. Gladys rebuked him, "I wonder who gave birth to you, and will be very troubled in spirit if your mind is filled with palm wine. Don't you know it will draw attention?" Sterling also grilled him rudely, "Have you taken leave of your God given brains, huh? Let your eyes light fire for you." All of them scolded him, "What is wrong with you? Are you okay?" He would have been lynched if he had moved an inch to try their patience. The Hunter was given a night optical device to aid his night vision. With a common nucleus to stay ahead of the curve, never to underestimate their opponents, erosion of legitimacy begins the moment capturing Animal. TORNADO was prepared to implement contingency measures manfully, aiming at employing a sharp axeof discontent at the root of law and order, before the VIPERS got the notice they were besieged by opponents ready to wield an array of offensive and defensive weapons. Digging an underground tunnel to the Castle was ruled out due to time, now proceeded to take wide range of measures against them, quickly to derail the prospects of reviving their hunger for developing intercontinental ballistic missiles. Pondering on the possible extinction of the VIPERS, they were also aware of endangering their lives. Their watches continued to tick away with inescapable regularity, as tension rose. On the way, the crew came to a location fenced with barbed wires. It was such a thrilling moment. Earlier on Monica had informed of detonating bombs planted in the ground and hidden. Only the VIPERS and Animal knew the safest route. It was carefully planned, such that its sound blast echoed far and wide to serve as a signal on impending danger. They found it hard to discover deeply into the brains of humans to figure out obscurity of dominance and wickedness during conflict situations and the attitude that got in the way of mutual understanding, when one is denied of his rights, and undermined by blood thirsty monsters who revealed their wings of authority. As the group kept moving, tracking devices were placed at vantage points to serve as the path of navigation, and for a missile to make a way into the heart of its destination with a remote control when the need arises. The missiles were fitted with electronic devices that enable them to find and hit the objects aimed at, a technology known to them. The TORNADO organized cameras at the perfect precision of image, keeping beady eyes on their activities. They also peered through the telescope and binoculars, tilted to suit their likening, while devotedly, eagerly, and actively, monitoring inch by inch, so as not caught off guard, switching places in order not towear out. The TORNADO had clarity of vision from the magnification of the lens. They never in any way underestimate their quest for vengeance; to belittle the potential of VIPERS.

Richmond adjusted the rangefinder on his gun to zero in on VIPERS. He kept looking through a pair of binoculars with critical eyes, to snap anything catching his attention, while at the same time, in conflict with an attempt to feed his eyes on stripped nice women, hence, drifting from the reason being there. Instead of focusing on the intended purpose, he allowed this Peeping Tom caliber to manifest on the battlefield. He is familiar with rules of being told, "You are fired!" On basis, he veered away from his focus. After all, he has his wife for himself as soon as mission carried out, and out of harm's way. He observed from a distance, VIPERS well organized, with their weapons entirely armed. They moved in groups, and fully observant, but as he kept watching, abortive attempt to divert the cause of action occurred. The ground quivered, and outstanding tower like a pole emerged. Its door opened. What he saw was very fascinating, causing alarming pain to his eyes. His eyebrows kept rising to show bafflement. He signaled to the Combat Contingent who had already noticed in astonishment. This led to an open passage dug through high ground connecting the Castle to the research laboratory. VIPERS came out followed by a truck carrying a rocket named, "the Destroyer", as if a new Armageddon story just about to emerge. The VIPERS took stance, highly vigilant and watchful. He then figured it was rocket or ballistic missile launch, an unprovoked belligerence. Within few seconds, combat troop also followed, carrying mutilated bodies, burnt skulls, and pieces of bones. The mutilated bodies charred beyond identification were tossed to the crocodiles, while skeletal bones and burnt skulls were kept in a mansion, safeguarded for posterity. These were considered wealth of treasured embodiments. With time, the crew planned to check what was in the mansion. The Combat Contingent had to act hastily to stop the launch. It was actually a highly sophisticated, intercontinental ballistic missile. The VIPERS really enjoyed causing harm. This time, it was targeted at the continents, one after the other, and was yet to hear in the news of the colossal bombardment caused, to watch humans running for their dear lives, buildings demolished, roads destroyed, and even polluting the air to kill more lives than imagined. Without knowing the basis of origin, the scourge of dispute among nations was obvious, just around the corner, as one nation might accuse the other. As the TORNADO was about to cut through the barbed wires, the Military Division, the EAGLES, assigned to the castle was also ready to take action. They owe each other allegiance to risk it all and lay their lives for each other on the battlefield. It was time to deal with the hidden detonating bombs and landmines placed on or under the ground. Either they have to lure the VIPERS to stroll around the area to enable them know the safest routes or to use their dogs, since bomb detecting devices will take much time. The TORNADO was even exhausted and headache cropped in with slight fever. Their wandering eyes frankly made out there could be awkward feeling of brutality that will be inflicted on the outcome of them being noticed if the VIPERS were lured. This forced them into misdemeanor by allowing fine intuition mindfully to determine itself on the result of the event ahead, on the most conceded, approved, and assured grounds. Working according to time, they kept vigil from dusk to dawn in order to deal with the problem directly, likely to avoid all efforts proving futile. The Special Forces took notice of the VIPERS on duty, the daily activities outside the castle and the sentinel at the watchtower, a carefullyplanned surveillance. They knew the City of Casa will hardly yield to pressure, therefore would take them by surprise. Ready for the consequences, as anger, which breeds violence and hostility boiled over, while frustration generated wildness and cruelty. Keeping in mind hasty decisions will endanger their own lives, focus was fully observed on constant awareness. They had to act quickly to divert VIPERS attention, creating the impression of just stray animals roaming around their territory, really, a brainy attitude, trying to avoid the tendency towards a devastating blow to their lives. The TORNADO threw balls, while they let go of the dogs kept on a leash with mouths covered. The bombs blew up at precise spots, exploding in grand style. It shook the ground as experienced on an earthquake situation. Immediately, the VIPERS patrolled the area, only to meet in outer dismay, dead dogs torn in pieces. As the VIPERS tried to fish out intruders, the lions with them, on the prowl, were left to feed. After strolling along the outskirts of the area, they left to their post while the Combat Contingent held them at bay, fully waiting for the right time to surge forward. The TORNADO indeed managed to outsmart them, but remained circumspect to their dealings and prudent as their eyes were strictly kept on guard, focused in all directions, aimed to act flawlessly, on the notion, the slightest mistake to lose focus would cost dearly, paid for with their lives. The lions had not finished yet with their feast. They made their day, never wasted a jolt of strength at all to have their prey, and extended their tongues both anticlockwise and clockwise as if licking their jaws from a sumptuous daintiness. Tension was rising. Time was also running out, as the Special Forces now considering the thoughtful idea to spot out and avoid pitfalls that ensnared them. With a technique to correspond, communicating by gestures, including sign language, and symbols, demanded absolute concentration. Obed cleared his throat to ease the critical phlegm in his voice, smoothing his esophagus. Probably the lion's ears caught a whisper, and noticed them. Notorious for agility and vigor, its spine-tingling roar smashed to smithereens the magnanimous silence of the wind, then growled and lunged forward. As usual, lions operate by isolating the weak from the strong, stalking its victim. The

Combat Contingent wanted to give those couple of shots for a toast. A wave of boldness swept over them, compelled to defend themselves. They dashed for action to confront what seems to be an insurmountable situation, and endeavored to be victorious. In a life and death situation, leniency is a thing of the past. Advancing in much coordination, they grouped in circular form with swords drawn and pistols held accurately, moreover, ready to situate their bows and arrows. All their guns had silencers. TheTORNADO adopted new strategy to scare the hell out of them by screaming angrily, and so loud. This seems to deter the lions from attacking. Yet, the lions gathered courage, as if playing chess in their movements; they bunched together and got fierce to maul its prey. Catherine wanted the bullets to go straight through the lions and that will be a time ripe for shooting spree. She aimed at them and opened fire until emptied out of bullets, then started to reload. Out of nowhere, a lion made an attempt on her, lunged forward ferociously, and energetically pounced on her. Catherine lost her balance and fell. The armor saved her. The lion grabbed her by the rib to sink its teeth into her, trying to pierce her with its fangs and claws that almost cut into her flesh. Peso ran through the lion with a sword, killing it in the process. TORNADO advanced toward the Castle. Approaching the VIPERS, their bodies went close to the ground, using their knees and elbows to push them forward. At a point in time, they lay on their stomachs with guns held, or a leg knelt while the other crouched, until was clear to advance. Moving in groups as they surged forward, the Forces slew the VIPERS to disintegrate their formation and authority. The battle cry seized the air. VIPERS were cut down at close range due to the proximity of physical recognition hardly confined in outward boundary to obstruct visibility, firing on all cylinders, ensuring of hardly any survival. Working according to time, the TORNADO announced of progress to the EAGLES parachuting to the castle. At every precision of advancement, all the Divisions ensured, at every specific location, on time, to have about three Special Forces assigned to a VIPER confrontation. The TORNADO managed to outwit and avert the VIPERS on the verge of launching the missile by inflicting severe casualties on them, and then deactivated the explosives. They wished to purify theminds of the VIPERS from destruction and violence, making conscious effort to eradicate all thoughts that were inappropriate in their lives, as they have been molded into ruthless and impetuous people, and their behaviours sounded very horrendous. It was a tremendous effort displayed by the Combat Contingent, aimed at bringing liberty to the citizens of Casa City, to undertake the full fury of vengeance against the VIPERS, as they fell slain. The TORNADO mingled with the indigenous people, dressed like them without recognition, and now wished to complete their assignment, have a nap, wake up, and crawl out of bed to face another day, making the best use of their time to achieve productivity. The pursuit of victory hardly succumbed to the demand for food, starving themselves to the last drop of saliva spat, only to unleash heavy shelling until the VIPERS could not stand their ground. There was active involvement to a vigorous resistance,never to invade with an all-or-nothing result, but an all-out outcome.

6. CASTLE ON FIRE

Christopher flew the plane above the Castle at a very high altitude. He is the Pilot flying the Military Crew known as the EAGLES to the Castle, conscripted into the Military as a Secret Agent. Listening attentively, the Crew was ready to parachute straight on top of the building. They had to show acts of bravery, as to carefully Pilot safely and quietly, ready to face the inconvenience of priority, and to put up with the difficulties ahead of them. It takes great deal of stamina to reach endurance, and at the end, it might sound laudable. The EAGLES believed in instant justice, crushing their opponents by any means possible with more fierceness, lashing out assault nearly out of bounds, and to vandalize all hidden doors of the castle, looking for clues and likely survivors. As usual, the VIPERS at all checkpoints on the lookout at rooftops, attentive to any intrusion, to shoot if the unexpected happened, and took turns to shield all fortifications. The Paratroopers airdropped with credible demonstration ofskill and far-reaching knowledge, and then went skydiving with altimeters fixed to their costumes. The Castle was clearly visible in the air as the Crew launched air strikes. VIPERS on guard then shot before the crew landed on the roof and on ground. Seeing a chimney on the rooftop, they inspected if it belched forth smoke, then, the Air Crew dived through, in single file and landed on floor pavement. Others had their way by ropes tied on the roof to the windows, melted the iron bars. Those on the ground were on the lookout;quickly overpowered the guards at the gate after luring them with noisy sounds when they opened to sneak around. They took their places in their uniforms. Others managed to climb over the wall. Moving cautiously and stealthily, they drew their pistols with silencers out of their holsters. There was an enormous space with numerous rooms and tunnels. The EAGLES threw smoke grenades, which suffocate the lungs and slightly obstruct vision, andhad their gas masks on to protect their noses and eyes, highly cautious. Aware of the upshot of interference, they overlooked the belief; sense of direction was non-existing, erroneous, and misleading, making sure to act perfectly and accurately. Advancing on instances of brevity, the EAGLES searched every room for Animal; they went on the offensive, firing in quick succession to outsmart the VIPERS. Fierce struggle for survival began. They fought the VIPERS furiously, charged with such ferocity for vengeance. A

Militant nearly inflicted with his sword. Adansi hurriedly shot and disarmed him. The Militant rolled to the floor on flight of steps. Their zeal not to accept defeat gave strength to their muscles. In one of the rooms, a Militant hid behind the door, knowingly, Chica entered in circumspection, got him by shooting through the door, watching upwards, downwards and sideways. The EAGLES also made use of their knives when they caughtsight of any VIPER, by skillfully throwing in an attempt to bruise the rib or poke the forehead. Coming within reach of a particular door, the EAGLES prudently made out Animal hid in there. Opening the door, the crew quickly forced a Castle Guard unconscious into the room, using him as human shield; Animal quickly shot at him until he emptied his gun, and then realized he was his own. A girl rushed out of the room naked, pleading, "Please don't kill me. I am paid for my thirst quenching service." Actually, she was then busy with Animal's head in her mouth. The EAGLES stopped her from escaping. She might blow alarm. The Crew then entered, two rolled on the floor and shot at Animal. He was weakened and it will take some time for the drug to send him into and out of coma. The crew poured petrol in the castle. Burning the castle should not have taken place anyway. Valuable assets must be kept for future generations. They immediately looked for the safest escape route to the sea, while Officers in the Navy arrived with speedboats to a location out of harm's way for helicopters. Then with Animal's phone, the EAGLES contacted VIPERS, whose names were on list, to meet at the castle's dungeon, locking all doors, only to provide a vantage point for their entry. Those called were his top officials. They were surprised on Animal's decision and hardly suspected of his capture. The EAGLES watched closely as Animal's Officials, his special advisors, trooped in like cocks after a hen, but led to the slaughter, and they killed as they entered. Unfortunately, time was running out, eating into a missile strike by a jet fighter.

The EAGLES cannot escape the missile drop if they wasted a minute. They instantly dived into sea with Animal and swam to the speedboats. However, the VIPERS in the submarine alerted VIPERS in the underground laboratories who with rapid response, marshaled troops. They took stage with their artilleries to thrash them with fury. Thunder, a Pilot from Salt City, was called to react with all his skills. Flying at the speed of sound and lightning, he launched an air offensive, and dropped air missiles, shattering the Castle and VIPER strongholds, which swallowed up in flames. The missile strikes took Casa City unawares. The sky lit up, consumed in thick smoke. Austin arrived with a chopper, which took off from the helipad, and lifted them to a place near the Prison. Hydroplanes were also available in a sealift. Capturing the submarine took place by the Navy at the time the paratroopers invaded the Castle by airdropping. The Officers dived below the surface of the ocean, wearing rubber suit, flippers, and special equipment consisting of a container of air carried on their backs and tube through which to help them breathe, intended to interdict immediate assault. Those in the submarine were unaware when the Officers charged on them, killing them in the process, and taking control of the submarine. Casting focus at a distance, The EAGLES with their telescopes and binoculars, observed vast heap of ashes, as smoke spewed out from the Castle. The VIPERS were totally vanquished, and taught to swallow pride, have a feel of the harsh reality of life, how to change it, and to learn humility. All in all, all were all laughs.

Personality is a source typifying our identities, in addition, to ensure we are hardly deficient of money. Inappropriate caution is misfortune to insubordination. The sky overcast, as cloud covered the sky. Thunder blast echoed its presence in the skies with lightning. Howling of the wind swept across the area, causing havoc with supremacy. Leaves of trees were smoothly swaying in the breeze. The rain set in and fell heavily.

7. EXECUTION

Prisoner's complained of the food making most of them sick, detested it when served, insisting on nutritious meal, but the Wardens sounded unconcerned, as if had nothing to do with such matters. The Prisoners signaled their discontent by refusing to eat. They were calling for a well balanced diet. Eagerness for sovereignty in their vulnerability rang bells in their ears. The yoke of repression was severe as the Wardens with iron teeth tightened their grips. Sudden panic ran down their spines when the thought of decapitation flashed their minds. For how long will they endure the most of torture? Nevertheless, they stood strong, and consoled themselves in hymns. On one occasion, Sean, one of the Scientists heard an awkward sound late in the night. The atmosphere sounded so odd to him. It dawned on him something was wrong. The oddity of the place was a hint of menace. Following the sound, he saw a creature with two heads devouring a prison inmate. Splitting headache struck him. His hands clasped behind his head. As he kept his gaze in astonishment, bewildered by what he saw, the man-eater disappeared to a steamy oblivion and the agitation subsided. Terror plunged into hysterics, and more than ever, now longed for redemption. As usual, when you cannot bear obnoxious behaviour with patience, you need relocation. In the morning, Sean narrated the incident to his Colleagues. They talked deeply into the night. This solved the puzzle of the missing prisoners that hunted their conscience. Carried out one at a time, a prison inmate, when seized during the night, had his head covered, handcuffed, and fed to creatures. The next night, the groans kept echoing. Honestly, nothing moved these monsters;the only thing to scare them was their own appearance when mirrors held in their faces. The guards intentionally released the creatures at night to kill, with the intention to decrease their numbers, before facing the deadly zone, which is guillotine. Their tactics were to debilitate their opponents, mainly to devitalize their judgments, to monitor their tenacity to startling situation, in order to surpass reasoning. A creature invaded one of the cells, and found Amanda. As she looked on, puzzled, the creature tore down the rod bars of the cell to meet face to face with her. She must face her fears considerably. It was then the Scientists caught a glimpse of the sickening sight of the monster, very terrifying with horns as that of a buffalo or rhinoceros. Breathing profusely, it held her and shoved her a distance away. She slumped on the floor as it flung her, and sustained injuries. The creature advanced towards her. She is now forced against her will to defend herself physically to keep her alive, bursting with ideas and inspirations to face all hindrances. Amanda aimed for its eyes and pierced it with her fingers, but she was bruised by the claws. The creature groaned as blinded. It wobbled, lurched forward, swayed back and forth. With the torn iron bar, she quickly runs through the creature, killing it in the process. The monster vanished. She could hardly guess what sort of creature was that. However, she has a story to tell, perhaps on these genetically mutated species. The T.B.A. knew the battle for survival has just begun, but lack of strength was not likely to see them through this hard time of their lives, wishing for divine intervention, perhaps remembering any Saint held captive in Prison during the primordial era. This time, those Saints are more contented in heaven. Even, some of them thought it was an illusion, seeing visions, and perhaps in a trance, where their spiritual bodies being set free from the taunt of bondageand the chains of predicament, sorrow and affliction.

The COBRAS had situated tank seized from the VIPERS hidden at length to the road, linking the prison and execution site, after laying ambush on them, and with carefully calculated scrutiny and exactness, aimed their weapons at its targets until justice prevailed. The COBRAS carried out investigation of the area, lying in wait, and took up conceded standing. Mindful of the VIPERS, but unknowingly by them when they least expected, Snipers hit them, and shot on sight. Massive operation ransacked their grounds, paving the way for an onslaught, and swiftly mowed down by the COBRAS after crossing River Jaina. Accepting actuality, it is risky to have any survivor in the river, the VIPERS never bothered to make the rounds, a scheduled tour of duty. When the FALCONS arrived at the very dangerous zone, River Jaina was full of crocodiles with long steady looks for defenseless prey, unperturbed by the zeal, presence and shrewdness of snakes and their deadly fangs. Snakes had shed their skins on the coast. There was no boat around. At that moment, the only way out was to swim. The onus was on them to derive the way out. Ega and his contingent had to evoke a plan. If the Paratroopers in a parachute drop had got to the other end, they would have endangered their lives. Satellite and radio communication reached the Military Divisions. An effort was made to locate the ford of the river. Frustration escalated. Simon told his colleague to swim in an attempt to take in his version of events. Sidney took it cool, smiled and started swearing, then answered, "Why keep a dog and bark yourself plucky chap? If you can swim in a river, never take pride in an ocean. I know you will not act foolishly. Their flesh is not like ours, and also do not think like us." Simon reacted, "Then, why do you eat their flesh?" Sidney answered back, "This is because I am omnivores, but not a cannibal." "Let sleeping dogs lie. We cannot eat and sleep with dogs, horses, and animals. Can't you see that buddy?" Simon said. The COBRAS shot birds flapping their wings as they flew and skimmed along the river, since birds are normally found at the bank of a river. As far as animals are known to crave for food, wherever there is food, you will find them almost together, and then supremacy takes its course. The strongest dominates. This was meant to know their number and if possible for the crocodiles and snakes to be led far away, feeding them with the birds. The COBRAS filled balloon boats by blowing air into it, as life rafts used as boats to cross the river. The FALCONS managed to cross the river to outflank the VIPERS at all angles. They waited vigilantly on the convoy.

At the prison grounds, a Warden addressed them, "This is your last chance to call on your God in prayers. The minute we turn onto the road, you already know where we are heading to." Penal servitude at times perpetrated acts of wickedness, especial on the grounds of transparency and blameless claim. The Scientists then knew the inconvenience to put up with the Wardens, almost a remarkable force to reckon with, and now misconstrued the relevant position of their articulated moment. The Scientists intentionally shouted when praying, "God, please help us! Let their morning turn into darkness. May their malicious thoughts entangle them like thunder strike, thwart their mischievous ways. May the demons of their great grandparents cease to hunt, and may their manhood swell thrice the size and quadruple... (started fumbling) err... err... o..." A Warden shouted, "Hey! Hey! Stop! Stop! Enough... ah! What sort of prayer is this? Echo, so you want our manhood to swell thrice the size and quadruple, eh? It seems you love to lick problem. Are you cursing us? Oh, please, spare me that. It is not surprising we had no pity on you when we turned a blind eye to your plea. We shall see what will happen to you." The Wardens handcuffed the Scientists and asked them again, "Is that how to pray?" Although the VIPERS acted outrageously, at least knew God not pleased with such prayers. Thanksgiving and worship commence prayers, and that with a clean heart, mind and in purity, then, subsequent words aligned with the Lord's Prayer. The patrol wagon quickly hit the road, shortly escorted in convoy by notorious Syndicates, heading towards the guillotine. A Warden stared at them, held his beard, and twisted the hair into pen. The Scientists felt acute nostalgia of endless confusion to faith as their hearts pounded, trying to gather courage, and carefully thought what at all sympathy meant. Moving towards their domain, telescopes captured the movement of the tumbrel. A tank drove in place and stopped on the road, ready for interception, just inthe nick of time to ward off any disaster. The tumbrel grounded to a halt at the sight of the tank. Silence means concern. The one in the tank stood upright and waved, disguised in a guerrilla uniform. Headlights were on full beam. The driver in the tumbrel came out, heading towards the tank, boiled with rage. Unexpectedly, the one at the tank discharged his gun. The tumbrel and those in convoy came under fire, firing in quick succession and precision. One of the vehicles pulled out and reversed. The T.B.A. took cover. Ganja held the bazooka on her shoulder, and then fired at the convoy and the tumbrel. The blast sent cars up into the air. It ripped off the vehicles in pieces with the tumbrel targeting the tires, for the sake of the Scientists, who escaped the accident by a hair breath. The Wardens felt dizzy. The FALCONS at the spot took control, drilled their swords into them and the blood stained the sword. The Scientists were giving tissues to blow their noses, assistingthe performance of their lungs to calm themselves down. The presence of the Military had a reassuring influence as they wept hysterically. Fizz of hope won them over. Their freedom began an era of bountiful happiness of the most glittering moment given to them, which was rather unexpected, and an uncalled for verdict on their lives, to such a deep sense of shock and grief likely to send down the spines of all in such situations. This time, the judgment and decree leading to execution now fell on Animal. Fleming floated the whirlybird in the air, and then touched down. Animal, when handed over to the Forces, covered his head with scarf, gagged his mouth that almost chocked his glottis, and headed towards the execution site. As his face was covered, the world seemed to be losing the visible brightness of the day. Aha, it serves him right. Vanity of destruction and sacrifice never lasted. Everything looked dim, murky, gloomy, shadowy, and unclear to him. The onedescribed as the strongest, skillful, powerful, secured, fortified, and proud, that same pride and boasting of his military strength led to his downfall. His empire was totally broken. Far back in his mind, his own shame only just imagined suppressing his irritation. A wave of nervousness swept over him, a dying need of emptiness consumed him as he realized the pain he had caused others, and thought of what reasons when spoken of him when he is no more. He was humiliated to withstand the worst, and conquered. Perhaps, the world will be better without murderers who have no pity on people, and very spiteful. He was so irritated, as if overpowered by some malignant force. It never crossed his mind he would end up this way. Now a terror to himself, he acted with urgency to return to the world of the dead, to extend greetings to them and taste if that place is also appealing, engaging, charming, and adorable.If he never knew eh, tell him the dead speaks a language unknown to the living. Likewise, Heaven also has spectacular language. His icy eyes went blank. His strength seemed to deplete. Animal tolerated his throes until his death. His executioner went through the same nightmare. Long awaited anticipation arrived, wanted dead on arrival, at the hunt of facing the music. The EAGLES, COBRAS, and TORNADO recited his guilt trip, "You have committed capital offence, one against humanity. You are charged on the grounds of homicide, massacre, accused of genocide and crimes against humanity. You never treated people like yourself. Even your name attests to this fact. So we give you what you deserve, a slaughterhouse. Those who kill by the sword, die by the sword, an eye for an eye, and a tooth for a tooth. Your judgment day ends here" The troops were now vindicated of killing him on that statement.

While blindfolded, they tied his hands to a tree and brutalized him with deep cuts and kicks on his body. Animal's hands and legs were shot. He bled from head to foot. Before taken to the guillotine, he was tied to a truck and dragged. The command went, "Finish him!" At once, the Executioner released the cord, and just in the twinkling of an eye, the blade of the guillotine cut his head off, beheading him instantly, finishing him off with the execution, for such a day of reckoning and the end of his numbered days. Blood streamed from his neck, and spattered on those standing close. The execution went on peacefully, smoothly, and perfectly. Judgment took its cause and got drunk of the slaughtered. This time, asking for legitimate reason to evil is instant justice. Mission accomplished. Out of sight, out of mind will be the lingering note of a saying. The next day, rumor went rustling around, spreading like wildfire. There he was, slain and lying bear with a headless body, decapitated and blood crying out in pain. The so-called, Mighty Papa was no more a terror or law unto himself, not at all to leave behind a flock without a Shepherd, but to pave way for an ordained Son of Man. The place was heaving with people to catch a glimpse of him, wanted to be sure of his death, to see is to believe. A very upsetting wakefulness of large sightseers looked on the decapitated head and body, hurled insults at him, cast slur on his personality, and heaped scorn on him. Infuriated crowd jeered the end of his sordid past, until the next day. On this note, a holiday was assigned to his celebration. Gloom hung in the stifling air. What an unforgettable period. There was no need for mourning, nor his sense and experience available for anybody to tap. Unfortunately, Animal became the receiving end of all predicaments when negatively branded. His special aids, close allies, top VIPERS, have all perished. Most of his combat troops were no more. Mega victory called for jubilation. These onlookers now have the guts to cheer after years of pain in the neck holding the City. Animal perpetrated acts of wickedness on his people, with severe persecution, a pleasure to see others suffer and gloat over their weaknesses. Obviously, he felt the pinch of his misdeed; the action and inaction carried out under his auspices. The storm now calmed in the midst of raging deluge of challenges. The Citizens enjoyed his death as they held no brief for him, keeping vigilance on the next leader, expecting him to be on the same wavelength of a Leader to serve his Citizens, giving them their heart desires and ready to listen to their requests. In addition, have the temerity to lead shrewdly and have Casa City at heart, to govern with diligence, solving the needs of his citizens. Citizens were advised to be vigilant and suspicious of anyone, acting as each brother's keeper to inform authorities of anything fishy. The Combat Contingent was firm to subdue and take absolute control of Casa City. Now, the full force of the Military might on standby, advanced towards Casa City, assuming command, and exercised full sovereignty, tried not to assign any breathing space for resistance. Their presence was an oasis of grand autonomy for the Citizens. Troops combed the area until not a sole left in sight, of those posing a threat, and eventually surrounded their territories. The smell of casualty infused the City, although the yoke of oppression was squashed and lifted from the necks of the Citizens, and were now led with cords of love. The rod of the wicked was thoroughly demolished. As far as the company of VIPERS posed a threat to global security, Military interception was justified. To the finishing line, the heat of combat swept away the VIPERS. The citizens at that time were addressed of the intention to intercede on their behalf and the need for their heavy presence, to let peace have a period of influence, and their freedom rated valuable; the freedom from theshackles of repression, misery, and destitution, to pave the way for their voices heard on issues of necessity to them. Social equality and the respect for human rights marked a new dawn in Casa City. The VIPERS were too full of them, and filled with smugness about defeat, relying on their armories. Casa City now stepped back from the edge of an abyss to spring into a moment of recovery, now time to amend the devastated City, with drastic measures outlined to help the ailing economy. The Citizens, with jolly minds, were surprised at the Forces act of compassion on them, ending hostilities, considering how aggressive they were. They were very grateful to the Special Forces for Animal's death, and for reaching out to the indigenous people cordially. Repressive regime now repelled on attempted infiltration, and law revoked to maintain law and order. The citizens were offered financial, practical, emotional, and moral support, as they took a stand to straighten their paths, a turning point in their lives. Straight away, they took onto themselves to build the City. Now, what is the point for violence? Faction of despotism was toppled to give way for stable government installation. Military presence took over air, land, and naval dominance.

8. WELCOMED BACK TO SALT CITY

All experienced sense of succor and liberty with energetic smiles transforming their faces, as they could hardly wait to come to their final destination, a survival of resilience, and a time to heal wounded emotions. The Scientists ached to reach home, with oneness for peace and tranquility. Burdened with thought had aged them. It is never too late to rebuild their lives. They wiped the drop of tears trickling like perspiration that drenched on their faces. Their worn out souls were reassured as their hearts longed for Salt City. The Combat Contingent endured an onerous assignment. It was an eye-opening occurrence. Families were eager to meet the T.B.A., making loud noises, singing, shouting and screaming, as liberated by the Special Forces demanded reverence for such a historic day. The family of the woman who had the bun in the oven at the Prison was also welcomed. They took their lives in their hands, and were in the limelight as men of valor, hence deserving recognition and praise. The T.B.A. was flown to seek immediate medical attention, a time to remember how they kept murmuring to express impatience and discontent on how to have arrested the situation they were in, then. Every morning will be the birth of a new age, featuring, and pointing to the sterling assertion of freedom. The T.B.A. are nowforced to develop a remarkable open-mindedness to find a way out of insurmountable challenges, coming to grips with reality, gathering tangible, visible and concrete evidence, more precise, definite, and particularly on dealing with issues, having a heart indispensable for thought worthy to discern abrupt ideas. With stickers pasted everywhere, having inscription of welcome, Salt City cheered their return. As they tried hard to swallow every bit of emotion to trigger tears forcing its way out of their eyes, their families swarmed over them, embraced, shook hands and kissed the survivors, welcomed with outstretched arms. Even in the depths of despair laid victory, with an air of calm surrounding their relief from misery. The grim actuality of prison life was now thing of the past as agony, set free, envisioned total emancipation, with the liberty to live as humans. Hearing the sound of the radio on was with harmoniously tuneful songs, which softened deeply into their hearts. The President also welcomed the survivors; informed earlier of mission accomplished and the era of dictatorship subdued. Lively moments permeated the inward appreciation to see light at the end of the tunnel. The Combat Contingent had then ensured of stability in Casa City, bringing about political, social, and religious changes, giving way to freedom of expression, provided not to bring one into disrepute. After having managed receding commotion that ensnared them, the Troops were ready for takeoff to Salt City, exulted as conquerors to accentuate accomplishment, and left as sound as a bell. The aero planes lifted into the air until covered by the clouds. Hardly was any tremor going through them. Reaching Salt City, the Pilots received instruction from the ground for the airplanes to land grandly. When a Pilot was to land with more complicated procedures, few tips were; to pull down the yoke to keep the plane balanced, turned the trim wheel gently, pulled back the throttle until the nose of the plane dropped, pressed the plane's landing gear to the ground, held down firmly the decelerate button until the plane stopped. All touched the runway safely. Jasmine, Doxie, Shola, Cindy, and Christopher, to name but a few taxied their planes to safe spaces. A grin unfolded across their faces. Their return from line of duty enlisted rousing ovation, accompanied by cheers, and shouts, and received media coverage. Television crews were present to catch a glimpse of the Special Forces, and proceedings. The Television cameras were keenly on them for interview and pictures. The Radio waves ceased the air. Their work paid off at last, risking their lives for such unpredictable agenda to save. An avalanche of congratulation came from all around. Airlines opened to fly from Salt City to Casa City, anchored in an ambianceof peace. The close affinity of togetherness was endurance, as the Forces cast their minds back when sent to survey the land and assess their military capabilities, watching with keen suspicion, marshaling concentration, ensuring mission hardly spinning out of hand. In plodding along through their speculations to victory, at last, men of standing underscored the decadent conditions that played the remarkable route for reformation. Their efforts amply rewarded as men of wisdom, and hailed of gruesome interception of enemy aggression, aiding for things to return to normalcy. The President, bestowed on them titles, an insignia of ownership, for their remarkable bravery, boldness,resoluteness, confidence, and courage, honored in dignity, a mark of resounding victory, of eminent disposition. The President was then debriefed on what transpired. The President prepared the ground for peaceful transition, also signed a decree to declare Casa City anindependent Country with an elected government, and regularly held referendum on the constitution. In addition, he sought a well-healed economy. When new laws were introduced, existing laws unopposed were amended amicably. National and General elections were held, eligible individuals stood for office to convince voters who could cast their ballots. The winner was sworn in as President or Prime Minister. Subsequent winners also held their offices. The President or Prime Minister then formed government, cabinet and appointed his Advisors until he or she served his term of office. Head-on discussion often went on between Casa City and Salt City, advised on matters of governance, where, the President played a remarkable role to an immense development in the Country. Governance fell within the ambit of the rule of law.

Casa City was now on grounds of passivity. His declaration firmly put across much articulation of decorum. A row of medals was pinned to the breast of the Forces' coats, proven as achievers, a capstone of recognition for such demanding caboodle. The mission indeed went with a bang, thus, no more instances of injustice and obstinacy. Every activity commences with a reason. This forms part of our lives to influence our personalities. The world will be a better place to live in, if we see ourselves as a reflection in the mirror. The Tower of strength is the Lord. Casa City now planted on solid fertile soil, hard to unearth, when the age of internal strife ousted, and era of social ferment subsided. Cultural diversity was encouraged. Knowing the mind, a precious commodity to waste, Casa City was resolute to build their lives anew, kept a wary eye on whatever went on, as the watchtower hardly slumbers. All are well that ends well.

9. FAMILY MOMENT

Christopher knocked on the door. His wife and children checked on him on the CCTV (Closed-circuit Television) screen. He opened with keys, can smell pleasant perfume in the room. What a hectic flight he had, although he loves to fly above the clouds. Christie Betty drew near him. She hugged him and he kissed her. Her hair extensions fell flat on her shoulders, though, barely limited to her choice of style. On the virtue of family life, he approved of her countenance and observed her fineness; a month now, since she delivered a baby, now looked strong with adorable features. He wished to have her with passion and to organize festivity for his adorable children, a hell caring for them as he adopted an air of indifference. Caring for children all depend on your wealth. Money is normally the key. Also he teaches the children to bear helpful thoughts in mind and live a holy life, for it keeps the soul and heart alive and helps the children to become useful materials in society. A good deed is rewarded and withdrawal of reward for misbehavior and disobedience. The child then takes cognizance of good traits and embeds in the mind. In the course of life, what implanted in them serves as a reference to morally accepted behaviour. She was with utmost perfection of beauty and qualities all men wished women to have, and well groomed, absolutely, the perfect core of beauty. He admired her for sticking to her principles with an undeniably keen intellect. She was irresistible with her appealing and seductive powers, very attractive to feel for love. Christopher was very fond of her, propelling him to ignite the motive on a compromise to the brevity of being. He thought as a man, his life is incomplete without a woman, and spiritually, without God. Their intimacy had deepened due to the level of coordination and understanding. Love is full commitment, but not on coercion. In love, you put yourself in one's position. It is necessary to familiarize yourself with the mind of your partner by her conduct in words and deeds during courtship. Relationship depends on building a solid foundation of respect for each other, trust, honesty, harmony, love, sexual satisfaction, cordial relationship, a healthy lifestyle, and an expression of genuine affection. There is a cause for concern if discontentment crops up, noticing disagreement and conflict. In a case to foresee the far-reaching impact of disapproval that is not only on beauty, but the inner manifestation of beauty on how one conducts herself in all endeavors, each can decide if realistic to stay in the relationship or to wash hands off before marriage. When it came to the choice of a woman, he went in for the definition of a lady; a woman who is polite and well educated, has exceptional manners, and always behaves well. One with internal gratification of loving no matter what may. However, marriage is not only limited to the intellectual elite. As far as you live in a society, you are bound to learn its culture of laws, norms, values, and moral principles. This places the individual within the parameters of an educated entity.

Notwithstanding a society that lacks quality of knowledge subjects itself to a mind of slavery. Others dictate for compliance. It brings one to bear on strings of restriction hanged on the throat, such as a wind without direction. He checked her life since childhood to her present age to know her dislikes and likes matching his own, a woman of help, one you can count on no matter any condition, be it happiness or when the soul fumes in grief. These criteria act in accordance with marital fidelity. Even though most women look for men with lots of money, marriage of convenience, where it depends solely on what to benefit when money is available, seems not to last. The shroud to envelope a couple who can stick to each other while never ending is tolerance with reason but not pugnacious. There is no love when marriage is on false pretense. Men dislike unnecessary arguments having an advantage over marriage, as a result, being the cause of rebellion, violent or mildquarrel, and disrespectful behaviour. Men prefer sincere and courteous resolutions to a disagreement. In courtship and marriage, everything about the man becomes irritating to the woman when he cannot perform well in bed. The slightest grievance against each other will escalate abnormally into conflict, but when the man is considered very special with absolute necessity of complete energy in bed to enhance her reach multiple orgasm, then, difference of opinion is overlooked, and well thought-out an admiring compliment. She makes everything viable to keep the marriage alive. Being a devoted husband brings relief to the wife. The first impression a man reveals to a woman as a sign of interest tells of her beauty in his perspective. What to sustain a sensual feeling is her behaviour. He expects her to display extensive maturity in dealing with problems, to tickle his mind to higher heights in all activities, and always activate his capability toaccomplish a task. Most women also demand reverence from men, admiration, acknowledged as having high opinion, those men can look up to with maximum attention, and want to be valued. Nobody was born a failure, how then; anybody chooses what is unacceptable to the body. After supper, he will calm his mind to succumb to the hot deep-seated desire burning within, one of fancy. He was hungry and thirsty for her. On face-to-face moment, she was so confident and easygoing, with such oddity of style. Her presence thickened the air, with soft voice so majestically creamy of tenderness. Christopher sat in a chair, tossed his hands into his breast pocket, and out with a fat cigar, with a carton of cigarette at his side, a captive in smoking, but then saw Christie Betty looking intently in difference of opinion, although she also loves to smoke electric cigar. She interrupted him, offering him a scoop of ice cream he fancied. He stood upright, extended his hands, and with his palm, put the cigar and lighter near the television actually on with programs televised live. Christopher reached for the remote and started changing channels. After surfing the channels, watching what was aired, he went ahead, reading a book of each Country and currency. Songs with strong rhythm in the larynx, with a magnum opus of brevity, incorporating a crescendo and a diminuendo gradual and fast tempo, music with lilting melodies of tonality and lyrical blues lifted his spirit as he tuned in the radio. Music is life to the weary soul. He checked on a spiral display of earliest photo gallery and objects sculpted in the room, likewise his own bundle of photos snapped with family, at places of interest, and friends. He flipped through to observe the faces of childhood photos and clasped one to his chest. Dogs barked at the next house, and always growled, snarled, and bared its teeth at strangers. Life filled with unforgettable moments as his figment of imagination did brood over his past, then wrestled with his thought about facts and an intuition to figure high on his list of priorities. As a kid, he thought like a kid. Nevertheless, his level of thinking eluded him as that of an adult, but very smart to know he cannot be naked in public for girls to express amusement. His first day in school, the Headmaster asked of his name. He replied by saying he should ask his father who was then with him, for he knows his name. "Don't be silly, tell him your name. Use your head, son. Equip the mind for adult life. Act your age with wisdom." His father rebuked. He has come very far to confine his mood when indignant. Controlling emotions enable one to live at peace everywhere, but is advisable to stay away from those who intend to provoke. Assimilating the mind of a baby never abhors iniquity in heart. A baby neither knows what is right nor wrong. An irreversible past to correct mistakes will serve as a signal to think carefully how he administrates his ways, following the heart and mind in sound judgment. He recalled instances when a kid, the awkward, pleasing, and fascinating moments schooling, with the strenuous effort, burying himself in his studies, never wasted the tickling clock. Also time with unjustifiable indictment, and the period when he developed strong affection for the girls in school before Senior high school. Youth also have their challenges, always desperate and anxious to live in affluence, but unfortunately end many in unwanted situations with no escape, worse than before. At a younger age, his whole life seen through the lens of demystification lies before him, to signify how to treat one another. When old, he will think of firmly held beliefs, the next life after earth, exceeding our celestial bodies, to Heaven of course. Patience is painful to abide, but at its optimal limit always idyllic. He devoted time to scrutinize and analyze his life, struck the root course to identify achievable and unachievable deeds, and on how to address unmet goals that transcend every endeavor. Anything irrevocable to repress our emotions was ignored. Having solid and scholastic academic credentials with excellent results, the moxie for merit, was his center of attention, and all along stipulating that, making it in life required willpower to stick to clear-cut plans, steadfast in studying, and valuing time, by working round the clock as well. Wealth creation requires having to think new ideas, and then the requisite qualification, with skilled and experienced workforce an advantage, in addition, critical decision to get the masses and the end users. We grow old, where our physical conditions ebb away, only to remember time spent never got back, knowing there is more to life than expected, not only confined in bottles but to think out of the box. He never gave up, always hopeful to attain and actualize objectives held in high esteem. Ideas still crossed his mind, and he took a deep breath. As a child, his parents taught him the Ten Commandments, and he stuck to it, to avoid indulgence in criminal activities, fraud, forgery, and pride. He learned to walk in love, illustrate kindness, have patience, meekness, humility, as described in the fruits of the spirit. He took a long hard look at the ingredients for change within religious standpoint, coming to conclusion, lack of ethics, moral norms and values lay a world of anarchy. There was absolute quest for in-depth gratification to unknown and things absurd, spurred on by mysterious inquisition to the forces that held the universe in place, searching for the ultimate truth, connoting a constant drive to the manifestation of who God was and is. The inexplicable modality to monism and the mysticism on creation burdened thinkers. Feeding such thought once in awhile, made his mind sick for answers. In this, the Ancient of Days, the Infallible Persona, with unquestionable sovereignty was made known by revelation and vision to humanity, and was consistently involved in the affairs of mankind, by visible performance of miracles, signs and wonders by those He invested in, to divulge to those who seek Him, his mighty force to reckon, his underlying principle and will. Historical evidence lends credence to his immortality in reality. This was to acknowledge that God is a spirit and as the arbiter of creation, owned the puzzling fascination of the universe, and still is. His parents taught him to nurture and nurse reverence and total obedience to the Most High, the unseen God, and all the time stuck their oars in his affairs. In his pursuit of invisibility, he expunged every jot of doubting God, where the laws of science hardly identified, and only by abstract terminologies. He had reverence for different religious jurisdictions and their beliefs. From the time as a teenager, church was like a friend to him. Christopher loved to get involved in the sanctity and sacredness of the Lords Supper, worship, praises, preaching, and prayer. He had no doubt prayer can breathe a life into most desperate conditions depleted to the point of discouragement. Stirring sermon of a renowned Pastor, a Prophet and a Teacher, with in-depth exegesis, always echoed in his ability to remember a doctrine of divinity, "God is who He is. He treats us compassionately, remembering that we are made of mere dust and return to it at death. Learn to have the essence of working in harmony." Quoting from the scripture, "All scripture is God-breathed and beneficial for teaching, reproving, for setting things straight, for discipline in righteousness that the man of God may be fully competent, completely equipped for every good work." As the years run, we look back and take a stand on our lives, what accomplished and not able to. We will not continue to live forever. Therefore, let us plan to live the rest of our years in obedience to God and imbibed in the work of God, and of His word. Our avenue of access to eternal life is to seek our intermediary between God and us. The Holy Book tells us the attributes of God's name, who He is, and what He demands from humanity, for we find Him in his word. The decisive moment is to be set free from the bondage of sin that clouds the mind, which brings the human perspective to run contrary to God's own. What God intends for humankind is revealed reading his word to draw us quicker in our relationship with Him. Complete allegiance to Him will let us thrive in our weakness and the angst-ridden era that craves for answers to life,thereby hardly being at odds with Him. God in his infinite wisdom provided mankind everything needed for life, but disobedience corrupted its survival.

Human race inherited death and suffered due to insubordination. Sin corrupts the body as anyone stained with mud. A righteous life is to sustain the blueprint of holiness until judgment day, to overcome the shackles of sin. For God's perpetual Holiness invents a chasm between purity and sin. Who can endure the awesome power and bewildering spectacle of God's presence and seeHis brightness as an analogy with catching sight of the sun? He basks in a prayer appreciating we are thankful for everything. By crucifixion and resurrection, His Holy One atoned for our sins and drew humanity to God to prompt us to overcome and escape the desires of the flesh in order to inhabit in the divine nature of the Holy Spirit. Until we discern we have to live for Him, we are a miserable wanderer in a wilderness. Man and woman, as elements sanctified in the image of God must be treasured. In reality, you cannot count God out of desperate situations and decisions connected to the precepts of living. He calls for full-blown devotion to Him, by surrendering every aspect of our lives to Him and sticking to his principles. When life's storm begins to swallow up, his mighty hand is always geared up to rescue when we call on Him.

When we take God at his word in reverence and decorum, we personally get the message he could be counted on to save us out of volatile tragedy. He is the only one who gives order to amend the forces of nature. What legacy can we entrust to incoming and outgoing generations? Are they to meet and inherit memories of a world torn apart and into pieces out of the jaws of predators, or to welcome and comprise an age of propriety? In his word, God attests to the fact that he is a consuming fire. Look within you, and have compassion, showing love to all, helping each other to fulfill his life well on earth when there is a need. We should try as much as possible, not to speak and behave cruelly against those who we think our mental faculty does not match their brilliance, intelligence, and experience, whereby we believe our highly placed and educated stature, as we are, far exceed their expectations. We ought not to act as self righteous, having proud hearts and looks. Be careful of anyone who slanders, showing tooth in public to flatter, but hide much hate, deceit, and shame, talking, and spreading rumors often palatable, and attractive to hearers. They destroy the harmony, coordination, peace, cooperation, and goodwill among people, creating divisions among people and propagating falsehood. Normally, when you dig into the issue, you might conclude of grievances and extreme dislike as causes. Arguing with a hot-tempered man categorizes you as such. It is not nice to take the role of a fool when colliding over insignificant issues that can be settled amicably, but to only shun and retreat if no speck of reasonableness permeates. Arrogance should not be encouraged in a society, by demeaning others. We learn to respect each other. The saying, "No news is good news." Becomes meaningful when one gets scarce by changing environment to swerve the headache of worry when not wanted. Lifespan poles apart with marathon; it is not always a competition to live. Therefore, accept no argument to the contrary. Let the Holy Spirit get along with you, like a friend indeed." He was highly pleased, how the Pastor preached to ensure clarity is restored, but also recognized for his rebuking remarks, especially when he preached and saw a member sleeping, he calls to order. It baffles his instinct, intuition, and perception, what actually drive humans to believe there is a God. Uncertainty hangs around the mystical parlance of anticipation, astral realms of astrophysics, with different religions judging the existence of God, realism of prayer,resurrection after death, the deeper insight into the complexities to discern the true nature of the unseen God. He asked himself, "Are sufferings our own misdeeds or lack of a well-defined mechanism supposed to fall in place? Are we experiencing the mighty hand of God now, which was trusted long ago in the era of Saints and Prophets?" His instincts might force him to believe Spirit Beings really existed and even now, having power to kill. However, he held fast to the belief that, God was and still is. Many have faced challenges, persecuted falsely by their accusers, who never dozed until have pinned them down to the little drop of blood left in them. Others have been caught in the snares of occult practices, thus, not to underestimate the power of unseen forces. Contrary to where Christians have their limits when it comes to occultism to seek refuge in the Most High, who owns creation within the hierarchical order of celestial bodies. His altruistic demeanor was misconstrued as predicament, but he revived the spirit within to turn around unrealized potentials, gathering courage in the face of adversity, driven by the urge to work on every aspect of his life fallen short to a more refined state. In delicate situations, you act tactfully and carefully. Will children wait for misfortune to strike before they turn their ears to seek the source of living a fruitful life? One never denies the fact that, parents are supposed to play a protective role to take high quality care of their children until they can survive on their own. His Mother was an industrious woman, loving, caring, helpful, and of use. Christopher kept asking himself questions, "How are facts gathered? Where the facts well examined carefully and sincerely? Where they just based on hearsay or eye witnessing? How on earth will one turn to believe somebody, just saying something?" He tried not to stray from a straight path; the likelihood to getback on track was unfeasible. In the center of a chaotic situation is to find the way out. His useful life had been lots of pain with little happiness that in fact was incredible to adapt. He had few regrets which can't be corrected on time but never to be repeated, but strives for perfection, looking to the future with keenness to achieve his ambition, aim and aspiration, trying to complete every activity started, working on every aspect to a more refined state. There is always a price to pay in every endeavor, treating delicate issues with the needed attention, tolerance, careful thought, a sound pragmatic trend of decision-making, admirable sense of humor, and equilibrium of a calculated imagination. No doubt, at times, we ought to have clear indications of any decision for implementation before taking a step to authenticate its viability. He opted to yearn for change when conditions were terrible, craving for obvious piece of information as a stimulus to bring force tofruition, conquering limitations with precise solutions. Liberty is the gratification of freedom. Nonetheless, he cannot make it in life on his own. His success, help, and life never depended only on him. Top priority in life requires willpower, inner drive and those who hang around us with like minds, and are ready to support when needed, with words of encouragement and financially. There was no need for him to boast, but to be bold, swallowing his pride, to work in harmony, and abstain from selfish ambition; Focused in mind, to have desired result dwelling on charisma, individual consideration, intellectual stimulus, daring,dependability, flexibility, integrity, realistic dimension of objectives, judgment of priorities, and a time to turn the page. He estimated the time taken to complete a task, and working devotedly from start to completion, sequencing of tasks from the most urgent, having a strategic perspective, and coping with change, tobuild shared visions, and display personal effectiveness. Moreover able to identify the dynamic situation of a problem to solve, with far-sightedness, able to have desired results, focusing on change when urgent and it might help, awareness to realize what is more to life and potentials. In addition, to maximize reachable achievements, to have competency, which is the skill, knowledge and behaviour needed to be applied for effective performance to attain goals. To nullify his plight was knowledge acquisition, being one of the most expensive commodities one might wish to pay a price for, worth fighting for and risking life with. Priority in life is to look at first thing first, envisioned to an expected end. Reaching the apex and pinnacle of aspiration, good is never enough when better can be achieved, and better is not the end point when best can be clung on to, of a life well-lived. His sense of right and wrong always hunts him. He defied all the odds to reach his goal in life. Every difficult situation is handled with sincerity and care. Every traumatic event like what troops experience on the battlefield or the ordeal endured after war has dramatic side effect. This is the reason why it is necessary to slot in Psychiatrists, specialized to attend to Military Personnel, for them to undergo mind therapy, ensuring right sense of mind and absolute efficacy of drugs and medical treatment in place. Most Military Personnel, after war and during training, suffer from post-traumatic stress disorders, hallucinations, strange dreams, dementia, anxiety, and unstable mind. This condition might be treated by adopting activities of interest, then sticking to it, such as music worthy of songs with inspirational words. Also, watching movies, having the consolation of heterosexual intimacy, enjoying the sentiments of companionship with children, having enough rest, and laughing therapy. He has come very far in life,where eyes watch how you can overcome your difficulties. He dwelt on blueprint for long-term strategic plan. One difficult task to do as a kid is saving little at a time, to accumulate into fortune when matured, a means creating wealth, by spending prudently, cutting down needless costs, besides, his question is, what about family planning? If childbirth becomes a hobby, who will take good care of them? A saving plan for the future begins as early as the little money parents offer their children.

Being financially independent is a tough challenge, but a sign of making headway, as it requires coping with the strain of spending, thrifty in that aspect, and of course to build up savings consistently. Having not satisfying this condition is like a fish struggling to breathe out of water as most businesses normally experience its peaks and troughs. This is what Financiers look out for, in innovation, dedication, loyalty, and strength of mind to come to terms with the mastery of every endeavor,

idealistic mind, and pragmatic steps to sort out finances and investments geared to increase wealth and maximize profits. This provides an enabling environment for a firm footing in business technique preconditioned for thriving businesses. When strapped for cash, the face becomes nullified beyond recognition with the eyes feeling like coming out of their sockets and the rims, where one is easily upset with the least irritation to get on one's nerves. Money, being an indispensable and a life enhancing commodity is integral to survival, hence demands working industriously. Having young energetic mind, directing their course to expected end is crucial to development. Days idled away ought to be recouped into important ventures. Productivity yields high proceeds when significant pay, incentive packages, and motivation depend on it. Can he even overlook the well-known rule? The higher the price paid for a service, the lower the demand for it, and the lower the price paid for a service, the higher the demand for it, although there are exceptions, especially, those who patronize luxurious services.

Psychologically, this involves lateral thinking to a problem solving, guided by instinct to evoke logical plans providing a way out of unwelcomed conditions. Decision-making is likely to outlast proactively with people on the same wavelength. As the saying goes, "Necessity is the mother of invention." With a note of concern, one is obliged to turn circumstances around. We ought to be open-minded to diversity in knowledge acquisition. Ignoring bits and pieces of information are much more solutions, and panacea for an ocean of problems. Hey! We have all had hard times in the prime of our lives, but hard work pays a good timekeeper. In all things, we have to remind ourselves, if society thinks an act must be turned away from, or supposed to be appreciated.

Christopher smelled the pleasant aroma emanating from the food being prepared at the kitchen. He went to see her, catching glimpse of kebabs on short and long sticks, chopped meet and onions, sliced tomatoes, vegetables, fried chicken seasoned with pepper and garlic. Rice and Stew decorated with parsley were on fire and baking of bread in the oven. The onions stung her eyes as she blended the ingredients, building teardrops, and at the same time, kneaded dough for baking bread. In the course of cooking, she suddenly withdrew her hand by touching the hot lid. He brushed his teeth and bathed. She did the same before and after cooking. He laughed heartily after eating, masticating the food in haste. Christie, with perfumed sensual body, approached him and landed a kiss on his forehead. As usual, she was always available to fulfill an emotional need, very charming with the most noticeable and notable elements. He was amazed at the feminism of her wondrously embellished curvy dressing gown. Her presence created a perpetual brilliance, indisputable in completeness, incontestable, incontrovertible, undeniable, and beyond doubt, with hair woven in bunches. He struggled to remember the number of times opting for a time out at a beach resort with her, which she was hardly used to. She is pretty from the inside out, with a strong feeling of affection captivating to bones and marrows, ligament, cartilage and tendons, perfecting the sexual chemistry of attraction. He kissed her deeply with passion. Her lips maneuvered with the rhythm in his tongue, as his observation said so, with mouthful of air due to her heart missing a bit in his presence. His hands unzipped her brazier to expose her beautiful breasts. Her skin was soft and supple, having refreshing and stimulating burst of spectacular sensation of intensity, of a seduction for sexual enchantment, soothing her most sensitive persona. Herareolae were visible, stiffening her nipples attentively, and breasts increased in size. He sucked and fondled her breasts to feel the erotic arousal, moving his fingers over her stiff nipples. Her body mechanism elicited wave shocks, organs so sensitive to stimuli. Fulfillment of foreplay in time is leading to ecstasy. He undressed her eagerly. Christopher detected intently each nuance of concealed personality. He fastened his eyes on her in admiration. Oh, Lord, the Maker of Heaven and Earth, you marvelously formed one of these starry idols. Ocular fact never doubted his pair of eyes. The reproduction of an image signals and reflects what the human eye can see. This seems to stir the blood. Erection erupted smoke on his foreskin of elastic fat todger, strengthened with perfect potency, phallus of masculinity, a complete personal business for a room of blessing. Man of virility seems fully ready to discover. Her beads made with an artistic attractive decoration, beautiful to look at. She spread her legs out openly, felt very moist inside, and then remained calm to have him with such passionate affinity, unable to hide her feelings for how much shelonged for him. His eyes twinkled with much expectation as he entered her sexual reproductive organ with much perfection of skill and appreciation, then looked intently at her to read the beatific expression, as her eyes brightened with delight on her face. Sizzling in a trance, she frankly liked how he moved to and fro– backwards and forwards, so fast and screwing so deep calmly. Ouch, it hurts, but so exciting. She mentioned his name softly and with tenderness, one of gratitude. What a consensual agreement on a consensus, mostly to last. He was riding to the perfect sumptuous dish. He kissed her with obsession and she submitted to the fact that she wanted him more than ever, and was impressed by his performance while having her in diverse positions. Yeah, he did remember where he came from at birth. At a sitting position, the muscles of his lips were at work on her nipples. She hardly controlled her breath with short breath gradually getting longer, as overwhelmed with secreting inner sweetness. He kept reading her lips, uttering words of submission, with her face, drawing conclusion of purity and innocence. Her beauty carried his heart away, to a key torrid love article on obsession. They had the heart to have children. Where in heaven can you find such an indissoluble union? He fucked with emotion, certainly expecting this unison to last a ripe old age, until the eyes grow weak, where their beauties appear ageless. It was very exciting when driven with passion, sensitive eroticism in the cunt, and mutual consent. She went for his head, sucking with amazing affection to complete the joy shared by couple. What a sensation, a mind-blowing fellatio on him, a teaspoonful prescription. He assimilated into hierarchical romantic contentment, floating on air.

Sensory stimulation enraptured his sensitive organs, veins, and muscles. Heart's systolic tempo read very fast, increasing mightily.

Love with obvious obsession burns with intensity, discharged to its final abode, and although quenched, it rekindles with force to subdue realms to an act of soberness in tender care.

Irresistible tickling reaction built in his body. His vas deferens instantly activated as biological reaction went on, and, Lord of mercy; he saw teardrops, perfectly visible, seen of clear viscosity. Christopher was at climax. Reaching orgasm, he dispensed a healthy dose of nutrients in the course of insemination, when out with her. Similarly, Christie Betty's folds of skin moisturized from within. They cuddled up together with more kisses. His eyes lit up with a smile. Their eyes met with a grin for love, until both dissolve into laughter. He sought solace in her memory. She awarded him a perfect score. Soon, nature will have its place in the womb to implement a predilection for intercourse. Absolutely, procreation was in the galaxies, in the heart of the solar system. Quiescent impression resided in the air. Her face streaked with tears of joy.

Christopher was woken early in the morning by the noise of a baby crying as Christie Betty called him from the kitchen. He could hear the sound of flight of birds singing and soaring in the skies, the dawn chorus of birds in the morning. Noise and shouting interrupted his sleep as well. A cock crowed and preened itself. A flying vehicle flew across the sky. It was a dream. All what happened was a lasting impression so real, permeating his cephalic skull, as he entered his head on deep reflection. He had drifted into deep sleep, and all along, Christie Betty kept an eye on him, listening to him, as he kept talking in his dream, uttering words unconsciously from soup to nuts. She heard him say this Latin tag well known, "Si vis pacem, para bellum." (If you want peace, prepare for war) and also, "Si vis bellum para pacem."*(A leader who is planning a war should put other nations off guard by cultivating peace)* Then there was a knock on the door where she verified on the CCTV (Closedcircuit Television). He considered the dream deeply. Military intervention is easier said than done. Enormity of the incident etched on his memory, and kept surfacing for life. Every solution to a problem is preceded by a preconception, which digests after chewing, by forming a battling mind of opposing forces, until a distinct choice of action distinctive to fulfill apredestined course or agenda. Problems must be addressed immediately when they crop up. We are tempted to lack behind, listening to anybody who castigates with phrases such as, "You can't make it in life." Instead of finding solution to their shattering predicaments, they shift the blame and gloat over horrible situations, rather than accepting mistakes, taking responsibilities for any mishandled occurrences, ensuring unrepeated. Being of one mind enables one to get the picture of how to treat anyone. After all, we all have common sense at birth with which to grow, and there is no ground for contentment as a levelheaded person in every situation demanding improvement. Obviously, a mother who clasps a baby delicately will hardly let go of the toddler to fall, likewise how we tackle our life challenges, taking a decisive action, reflective of how quick to respond to our present situations. The very minute limitations that seem insignificant in futility to thwart our efforts might get out of hand, if countless attempts not made to arrest the situation. When conflicts arise, it should be resolved politely. He pictured the future, relying on his state of affairs, to either bleak, or bliss, and then focused on searching the ultimate purpose for his life. When in deep sense of dejection, he breathed in with emotion, and revived his spirit, never to give up, but move on withhis life. Trees adorned with lights spread out to cover the City with much embellishment. He opened the door with an inscription written on it, "CASA CITY," only to see dazzling morning sky. He contemplated on procedure to spell out the very yardstick that inspires untapped potentials, to be fully committed to a legacy to succeed, formulating ideas in his head, considering how to carry his life along on a reasonable opinion. We inspire to cross the finishing line in safety, to be abreast of significant improvements in our lives, with principal values to act as instruments for change. Reflecting on the inner man draws out the needed insights to discover ourselves. Christopher's thoughts went deep, as though his eyes never closed, but actively blinking. He kept asking himself numerous questions to find out the profundity, acme, length and breadth of the mind, and then measured the air in his breath. The time is crying out to open modern episode in his life, without getting rid of realistic past. Exquisite optimism thrilled his innermost consciousness. The unknown prediction about the future electrified eyes on fire, catching the throat and body in its entirety, instilled in him perfect inexplicable buoyancy, extricated from his current plight, desperate for change to unfold expectations. He was with the urge to insist on bold benefactors to stand in the gap, piercing the realm of accomplishment to breathe new life of fresh air, solution, victory, medicine and antidote for spiritual healing. Also to pacify, and resuscitate the cadaverous dead spirit, a phantom of illusion, that lived in paradoxically discordant perplexity, sick of decaying anxiety and dilemma of lost hope that called for concentration and change , and finally, to absorb the essence of existence from now until eternity.

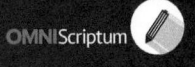